FORBIDDEN MATE FOR THE SOLDIER BEAR

SPECIAL OPS SHIFTERS: L.A. FORCE

MEG RIPLEY

SHIFTER NATION

CONTENTS

**FORBIDDEN MATE FOR THE
SOLDIER BEAR**

FORBIDDEN MATE FOR THE SOLDIER BEAR

SPECIAL OPS SHIFTERS: L.A. FORCE

1

Jude Sutton opened the front door of the Special Ops Shifter Force's headquarters, a sprawling Los Angeles house that he'd come to call home over the last few months. He was getting comfortable there, but that day, he wasn't sure how to feel about what was waiting for him outside.

As soon as he saw his brother Reid standing at the entrance, any doubt vanished from his mind. A short beard had grown out around Reid's boyish smile, and his dark hair brushed against his forehead. He was the same Reid that Jude had always known, and there was something comforting about having family nearby. "Come on in, man! I'll introduce you to everyone. Is this all you brought?" Jude indicated the small, rolling suitcase resting at Reid's feet.

"You know how I am. Always on the run, and I don't need much," his brother replied with a shrug.

"Yeah, I know." Jude was smiling, but that was exactly why he had some reservations about bringing Reid onto the Force in the first place. They were an elite group of special ops soldiers who also happened to be shifters, and they used their skills to help diffuse disputes among local clans. After all, most shifter issues couldn't be brought to the police.

Jude also knew that even though Reid was usually content to flap in the breeze, the Force would be a great place for him. "You showed up at the perfect time, you know. Everyone is here, but we won't start on anything official until tomorrow."

Reid rubbed a hand through his beard uncertainly. "Look, there are some things I need to talk to you about first."

"Just get your ass in here. We'll have plenty of time to talk. I promise." Jude didn't want to talk, because he had a good feeling of what Reid was going to say. He didn't want to be chained down. There was too much of the world to see, and too many things to do. Sure, L.A. was a busy place, but he'd tire of it eventually.

They stepped into the kitchen, where everyone had finished eating dinner and was cleaning up. "Hey, everyone. This is my brother, Reid. Reid, this is Gabe, Emersyn, and their son Lucas. Emersyn is our medical specialist, so you can see her when you have the sniffles. Melody, here, is our bookkeeper and takes care of Lucas."

Emersyn was busy getting Lucas cleaned up from his dinner, but she waved and smiled. Gabe strode forward to shake the newcomer's hand. "Nice to have you on board."

"Amar, here, is the Alpha of our group, and this is his mate, Katalin." Jude made a mental note as he introduced this particular couple that he'd have to let Reid know that Katalin was a vampire. She wasn't going to drink his blood or anything, but it was certainly something to be explained. The fact that vampires even existed had been unknown to them until recently.

Amar held Reid's hand firmly. "If your brother is any example, you'll be a great fit here."

Jude gestured at the couple sitting at the end of the breakfast bar, their legs and arms entwined around each other as they enjoyed a piece of cake together. "Raul, when he's not busy making googly eyes, is our tech guy. This is his mate, Penny."

"It's nice to meet all of you," Reid said.

"I won't harass you with all the specifics of our operating procedures tonight," Amar assured him with a glint in his eye. "We've got plenty of time for that tomorrow."

Reid was uneasy. He didn't need to say it; Jude could sense it. The two of them had been so close growing up that they practically thought like twins at times. Jude poured himself a large mug of coffee despite the late hour and gestured at the doorway. "I'll give you a tour of the house."

"What's up?" he asked as they crossed through the open floor plan of the massive living space. "I thought you were interested in becoming part of the Force, but there's obviously something bothering you."

Reid pressed his tongue inside his cheek. "I want to talk, Jude, but not here. Let's get out and go for a run or something."

Jude set his mug down. "Fine by me. Even working with shifters, I don't seem to ever get enough time in my bear form." They stepped out onto the back deck and skirted the pool, then Jude took a deep breath and let his human form go. His bear was always eager to get out, and there was something about the pain of shifting that Jude found pleasurable. He didn't mind the stretching of his face as it extended into a muzzle, or the pulling of his scalp as his ears lifted to the top of his head. The deep ache that came from the elongation of his spine and the shift in his joints only let him know that he was free. Then there was the tingle of every hair exploding from his human skin, and he was his natural state once again.

Is this safe here? Reid had also morphed, his bear still that same dark color that Jude remembered. His legs and underbelly were nearly black. Being family, they could speak to each other telepathically.

Absolutely. No one can see through these hedges, and we can slip out this way toward the national parks. There's a shitload of them around here. Jude eagerly led the way down the path and out into the wilderness. The sun had just set, and as lights came on all over the city, they escaped to the darkness. His muscles burned as he ran, letting out all the steam that had built inside his human form as he'd dealt with work and decisions and worry. In these moments, he could simply be himself.

They paused at the top of a rocky outcropping, where the stars were just beginning to wink to life overhead. Jude couldn't quite smile in this form, but he still had the same sensation inside. *You don't know how good it is to see you again. You're going to love it here.*

Yeah. Reid stepped out to the very edge of the bluff and looked down over the darkening carpet of trees below them. His inky coloring made him blend in remarkably well with the surrounding landscape. *What exactly is the policy on joining the Force?*

Jude felt his nerves stirring inside him. That was a feeling he'd often known when he was young, and it was only by keeping himself cool and calm that he'd been able to make it as far in life as he had. He wasn't going to let his concerns for Reid change that. *What do you mean?*

I know you pulled some strings to get me here, and I really appreciate it, but—

Don't do this to me, Jude interrupted, his own voice gritty in his head. *You were the one who called me. You were the one looking for the next step in life. Don't come all the way out here just to fucking bail.*

Reid was quiet for a while as he looked up at the stars. *You've still got that weird birthmark on your chest, huh?*

Jude turned away, letting out a huff of exasperation. While his bear was covered in typical light brown fur, a shade that closely matched his human hair, he bore the swirling lines of a helix in silver on his chest. It'd been one thing that Reid always liked to tease him about, even when they were younger. *Get to the point.*

I just don't want to make any life-changing decisions. I'm not sure what the future holds for me right now. If being recruited by the Force means staying with them for the rest of my life, then I can't do it.

Rubbing his shoulder against a tree, Jude thought about this for a moment. Reid had always been the wild one, the unreliable one. He'd gotten the two of them in more trouble than Jude could even remember at the moment. It figured that he'd want to know he had a way out, and it irritated Jude. *The Force has been one of the best things to ever happen to me. You know how tough it was for us growing up. I never had a good sense of family, but I craved it. The Army gave me some of that, but the Force has given me even more. I haven't regretted it for a second.*

So the dude in the Spiderman t-shirt is your brother now instead? Reid teased.

Raul may act like a teenager sometimes, Jude admitted, *but he's a stand-up guy. They all are. And the Force really does function like a clan. We have a strong Alpha in Amar, and we work well together.*

Reid shook his head, the movement shivering

down his neck and back. *I'm not trying to knock what you have going on here.*

It certainly didn't seem that way to Jude, but he wasn't interested in starting an argument. With a deep breath, he let himself fall back into his human form. Some things were easier to talk about outside his head. He sat and let his legs dangle over the cliff. "You've just got me worried."

Reid, also back on two feet, settled down next to him. "You don't have to worry about me, Jude. I'm not a scared little kid anymore. I'm a grown man, and I've seen combat just like you have."

"Easy enough for you to say. You were younger when it all happened, and you probably don't remember it the way I do." Jude looked off to the right, the images of those days as a child flashing unwillingly before his eyes. It was one of those things he'd tried to talk himself out of remembering, telling himself that it didn't really matter because it'd happened so many years ago. But it never worked.

"I remember," Reid countered. "I remember being at the Hoffmans that night, and that Mom said she and Dad would be back as soon as she could. And then they weren't. You certainly wanted to handle things, though."

Jude pressed his lips together. "I was trying really hard to be strong for you. I mean, you were my little brother. I can look back on it now and see that I was being completely ridiculous, telling Mrs. Hoffman that if she'd just give us a ride back to our house, I'd make sure you put on your pj's, brushed your teeth, and went to bed." He smiled a little at the simplicity of it; that at that moment, those little daily things were what mattered, even though they'd just been orphaned.

"I have no doubt you would've, too, no matter how much I tried to fight you on it. You've always been like that, Jude. I think you've been responsible ever since you were born." Reid's face twisted into a smile as he recalled their childhood.

Jude sighed. "You're right. Sometimes I wish I could let go of that, but I can't. I still find myself looking for the right way to do things, as if there's ever only one. I've got make all the right choices, ones that will still be right years down the road. I can't say it's been an entirely bad thing, though. It did land me with the Force, and I meant what I said about how good they've been for me."

"Right. Your family," Reid nodded. "I get it. We were dropped off with babysitters that ended up becoming our adoptive parents, and there's no denying that affected us. You've coped by trying to find a place to fit in, and I've mostly coped by trying to make sure I'm left out. There's no perfect way."

"No," Jude said with a frown, "but I do think the Force is the best option for you. You won't have to look for a job or even a place to live. You know you'll be with other shifters, so that means fewer worries about keeping your truth a secret. There's no better option."

Reid raised an eyebrow. "You're not even going to bribe me with the L.A. nightlife or how hot California chicks are?"

Jude elbowed him. "I have no doubt you'll figure that part out on your own."

"It wouldn't matter, because it wouldn't work anyway. I've met my mate."

Blinking out into the darkness but not seeing it, Jude wondered if he'd heard his brother correctly. He swung his head over to see Reid grinning at him. It wasn't the mischievous smirk he was used to, but something completely different. Jude couldn't remember seeing Reid look like that since he told him he was joining the service. "Are you serious?"

"Yeah. Never expected it. In fact, when our unit was sent to Thailand for some cross-training, I just saw it as a chance to see some new places. But then I met Mali, and my entire life changed. I've always heard people talking about meeting their fated, but I didn't think it would happen to me. It's incredible."

"Wow." Jude was genuinely happy for his brother. He'd felt that fated pull before, too, and it'd been just as remarkable as everyone said it would be, except he couldn't do anything about it. A pang of jealousy stabbed through his heart as he extended his hand to shake Reid's. "Congrats."

"Thanks, man. I actually brought her back to the States with me. That's why I'm concerned about committing to the Force. I'm not just making decisions for myself anymore, you know?"

"I get it. You should've just told me."

Reid shrugged. "Sure, but just blowing into L.A. and announcing that the rest of my life is being mapped out isn't really me. Come to think of it, settling down with a mate isn't really me, either. I don't know. I just thought it was better to say it in person."

"Yeah. Of course." Jude bit his lip, thinking about Annie. How long had it been since he'd seen her? Did she even remember him? There wasn't much reason for her to. It was yet another time in his life that Jude wished he could completely forget. God, it would've made things so much easier.

"I realize it wouldn't necessarily be up to you, but if I *did* decide to stay, would it be an issue for Mali to stay, too?" Reid's look changed from that innocent, 'I-hope-you're-happy-for-me' look to one of grave concern.

It made Jude realize that Reid was so much more of a man than the last time he'd seen him. Jude had worried when Reid joined up, just a fresh-faced kid who was determined to change the world. Apparently, the world had changed Reid, and only for the better. "Probably not. You saw that most of the members already have their mates here. We're all shifters, and we know how important it is."

"What about you? Haven't you found anyone to settle down with?" Reid asked. "I'm sure the girls out here are just falling all over you and your strong-and-silent-type routine."

Jude felt his brows lowering. It was just the way he was, and whether people liked it or not, that was their problem. But these thoughts were making his anger simmer just under the surface of his skin, vibrating down to his bear, daring it to come back out again. Getting into an argument with Reid wasn't a good way to make his brother stay, nor would it help his own mood. "No. Not really."

"Well, you never know. Like I said, I never imagined I'd meet Mali. I'll tell you the whole story sometime. And I can't wait for you to meet her. I think you'd really like her."

"I'm sure I would."

Reid pushed himself up from their perch on the cliffside and then paused. "You sure you're okay?"

"Yeah."

"I mean, I know we haven't been around each other much lately, but I do still like to think I know you better than anyone else in the world. If something's up, you can tell me. In fact, I really hope you do. I don't want you sitting here telling me it's no problem for Mali to be around, and then find out it is."

"No," Jude replied quickly, realizing he'd given Reid the entirely wrong idea. "That's not a problem at all. Of course, we'd have to talk to Amar out of courtesy, but I'm sure it'll be fine. I've just got a lot of shit on my mind right now."

"Okay. Well, you know where I'm at if there's anything you want to talk about." Reid hesitated a moment and then spoke again. "I should be getting back to the hotel and talking to Mali."

"Right. You go on, then. I think I'm going to stay out here for a little while."

Reid looked like he wanted to argue with him,

but the two brothers had always been pretty good about letting the other live his own life. When Reid had been young and particularly wild, he'd always counted on Jude to pick him up if things got out of hand. Jude knew that Reid would listen when his mind was heavy and he needed to unload a little. Their lives hadn't been perfect, but their relationship was about as good as it got.

Reid turned to leave, shifted back onto four feet, and lumbered off into the darkness. Jude leaned back and tipped his gaze to the sky, automatically focusing on Ursa Major. His mother had told him so many years ago that it was the first great bear, and the stars that composed it represented the spirit of all the bear shifters who'd ever existed. Ursa Minor nearby was just as important, depicting all the young bear shifters who were still figuring out who they were.

Jude knew, as a rational adult, that the constellations didn't really mean anything. They could be helpful for navigation or telling time, or even for locating a comet that happened to be coming nearby, but they were just random arrangements of stars. He still enjoyed looking at them and thinking of all the ancestors who'd come before him, even if he didn't know who they were. Somehow, people were always looking for guidance from the stars, even though it wasn't going to get them anywhere.

The chill of the night had seeped in around Jude without him noticing. Without his bear fur, it was starting to sink into his flesh. He got to his feet, cast one last glance at the sky, and turned for home.

Home. That was a term he'd struggled with. For most, home was the place where you grew up, where you went when the rest of the world had turned against you, where your parents were still waiting with open arms. For him, home had been many places across the globe. It'd been the Hoffmans' home, which they'd generously opened up to the boys. It'd been a small dorm room with little more than a bed and a bookshelf, and it'd been a tent that floated through the sands of the Middle East at the whim of his commanding officer. The house the Force had chosen as their L.A. headquarters was home now, but how long would that last? Would things change for him? Did Reid have a point about making permanent decisions? Jude shook his head. He didn't really want to know. He just wanted to be sure his brother was taken care of, and everything after that would fall into place.

2

ANNIE MARTINEZ STEPPED INTO THE KITCHEN OF HER clan's clubhouse, the place she'd called home for her entire life. It was a sizable kitchen, one that was more than capable of handling the steady influx and outflow of members as they came and went. It was always a place where the other bears could go when they needed a place to stay, whether they were waiting for the paperwork on a new place or because they were out of a job. The Martinez clan would always take care of their own.

But when she checked the large marker board next to the fridge, Annie frowned. "Jordan?"

No response.

She strode through the kitchen and poked her head into the living room.

Austin was slumped on the couch, his latest guitar in his hands, but he looked up and smiled when he saw her. "Hey, cutie. What's up?"

Annie inwardly rolled her eyes. She'd been ignoring Austin for years, yet he kept spouting off these ridiculous and degrading names as though they were going to impress her eventually. "I'm looking for Jordan. Have you seen him?"

Austin shrugged as he plucked out a few notes. "I think he's upstairs packing. Why don't you come over here and I'll play you a song?"

"Uh, thanks, but I've got things to do." She turned for the door.

"It'll be a good one, I promise."

Steeling her spine, Annie turned back around. "I appreciate the offer, but it's not really my thing."

His bright blue eyes never left her as he stood up and set his guitar on a floor stand. Austin advanced toward her, stopping when he was only inches away. He reached up and ran a finger along her jawline, his lips softening. "Annie, I don't think anyone in this clan really understands you."

Her gut contracted. "Why do you say that?" Austin was just not her type. He'd played in tons of metal bands, and his style fit the stereotype: jailhouse tats, under-shaved hair that was longer on top, and a ring through his eyebrow. He might have been hot to some women, but Annie knew how rotten he was at his core. She'd known him forever, and she wasn't interested.

"Come on. You're constantly making sure everyone else has what they need, whether you're making up a bed for someone who comes in off the street in the middle of the night or helping Jordan get a Christmas present for whoever his girlfriend of the month is. Who takes care of you?"

Ah, so that was it. Just some old bit, recycling a pickup line that had probably worked on some bimbo in his past. Austin was right that others didn't understand her, but that wasn't why. "I've got things to do, Austin." She turned on her heel and headed for the stairs.

By the time she got to the second level, Austin had plugged his guitar into his amp and was thrashing away. Sighing, Annie passed her own room and headed toward her brother's. The door was open a crack, and she knocked on it lightly before pushing it the rest of the way open.

Jordan looked over his shoulder and smiled. "Hey, little sis. What's up?"

Annie frowned at the clothes strewn all over the bed and spilling out of the closet. "I thought you were packing for your next trip. You don't even have your suitcase out."

"Yeah, I do. It's over there. Somewhere." He gestured at a cluttered corner of the room.

"Okay, then why does it look like a damn Goodwill tornado in here?" she challenged, picking up a silk shirt and deepening her frown as she studied the wrinkles. "I thought you were supposed to be some Hollywood hotshot actor. How are you going to go out in *this?*"

Her brother snatched the shirt out of her hand, crumpled it into a ball, and chucked it into a duffle bag. "Us *Hollywood hotshots* usually have lovely assistants that unpack everything and steam it. I don't have to worry about any of that bullshit. You should know that by now."

They'd barely started the conversation, and Annie was already feeling tired. She didn't like to see things done improperly, and an Alpha ought to feel the same way. But Jordan didn't seem to care. "I do know that, but I still think it sucks for you to take advantage of them. Those poor production assistants probably don't get paid nearly enough to have to put up with your ass."

He let out a bark of a laugh. "Annie, you forget

who I am! They're scrambling to come to my hotel room."

"I want to talk, Jordan. The last thing I need is another arrogant dick around this house." Annie shoved a pile of ties aside and sat on the corner of the bed.

"Austin after you again?" he asked as he moved to his dresser and hunted down a comb. "You know, you might want to give him a chance."

"Why?" This wasn't the first time he'd said it.

Giving up on the comb, Jordan moved a pile of books off a chair, turned it around, and sat in it back-ward. "Come on, Annie. At least just think about it. Agree to go on just one date with him and see how it is."

Annie's lips puckered sourly at the thought. "Oh, I'm sure it'd be *great*. He'd take me out to some dive bar where some asshole would spill beer all over me, and then we'd have a romantic time in the back alley while he tried to put his hand up my shirt."

Jordan rolled his eyes. "He's not that bad, Annie. I wouldn't even consider him as a possibility for you if I thought otherwise."

"He might not be as bad as I like to imagine, but that doesn't mean he's good, either. The two of us have nothing in common, and I don't feel that..." She trailed off. Annie knew what she was supposed to feel when she found the one person who was right for her, but only because she'd heard others talk about it. She'd thought she felt it once, but she'd been deeply mistaken.

"Not everything has to be permanent, Annie. A dinner together doesn't mean you're signing up for the rest of your life. I just think you could benefit from getting out a little. You spend too much time running around the clubhouse, trying to make sure every tiny thing is taken care of. That can't be good for you."

She planted a fist into the mattress. "Someone has to do it! Did you see the marker board by the fridge? I made it very clear that everyone can simply write down what they want from the store. If we're low on bread, just write it on the board. It's not hard, yet no one will do it."

"It's not that big of a deal. Just buy bread." Jordan noticed a pair of khakis draped across his desk, picked them up, and tossed them at the duffle bag he'd thrown the silk shirt in. The pants hit the side and fell to the floor, and he made no move to pick them up.

"You really don't understand, do you? I never know what I need to get from the store. I'm the only one who pays attention to what bills need to be paid. The house would've been sold for taxes if it weren't for me. Everyone just treats this place like it's some frat house they can trash whenever they want to and not clean up after themselves. It's like I'm the only person who cares about this clan!" She hated it when she got angry. That shaking feeling was too similar to the way she felt when she was nervous about something. It also stirred up her inner bear, which only made her even angrier.

"Hey, I care!" Jordan countered, swiping a hand through the air. "How do you think you're able to pay all the bills? That money comes from the jobs that I do, whether it's an action film or some hosting gig or whatever my agent tells me to do. I'm gone all the time, and it's for you guys."

"Yeah, that's right. Go ahead and play the martyr, Jordan. You sacrifice so much when you have to drive to the studio or fly to some exotic location just so the cameras can focus on your pretty face while you get pampered by half-naked women. Give me fucking a break!" She flopped back on the bed, wondering if her life had just been one big nonsensical dream she'd never wake up from.

A crumpled t-shirt landed on her face. "If you're going to cry about it, then just come with me. I'm heading to Vegas this time. You could have a lot of fun."

Annie chucked the t-shirt back at him. "Right, and just leave everyone here to fend for themselves. They might be grown shifters, but they sure as hell don't know how to manage the clan on their own." She took a deep breath, realizing she was getting far too angry. "Jordan, I came up here because I was frustrated with the house, but there's something I really need to talk to you about."

He rolled his desk chair a little closer, looking worried. "What is it?"

She sat up and folded her legs underneath her. "Jordan, you're the Alpha of our clan. I know you have this great acting career, but it's not fair that you're always off shooting on location. An Alpha should be home leading his clan more than anywhere else."

His shoulders sagged and he shoved himself up from his chair, tossing several more random items in his bag. "You know, you tease me about playing the martyr, but what about you? The only thing I ever hear is that you don't think I'm doing enough for the clan, yet I don't hear anyone else complaining."

"Like they're going to complain right to your face when they're thrilled just to be able to say they know you," she mumbled. Annie had seen her brother's face grace the covers of far too many magazines, and it wasn't special to her anymore. "I just think the responsible thing to do is to stay home and take care of the members."

He cracked a short, derisive laugh. "I wish you could see just how funny this is."

"What?"

"Annie, don't you remember what things were like when we were younger? Back when Uncle Jack was still the Alpha and you weren't so concerned about the job I was doing? You were always gone. You were out looking for trouble at all hours of the day and night, and I was constantly worried about you. When I did catch up with you and tried to say something, you'd just toss some hateful words at me and leave again. You sure didn't want me taking care of you, yet you come to me now and say I'm not taking care of everyone else." His handsome face had transformed from that of a carefree actor to a pissed off Alpha.

It only angered Annie even more. "I was a kid, Jordan. I was just old enough to get myself into trouble, but still young enough not to want any guidance. Not from you or our parents or anyone else. You can't still be holding that over my head."

But Jordan was on a roll. He picked up a pen and tapped it against his other hand thoughtfully. "What's even more ironic is that you don't want to have anything to do with Austin, yet he's exactly the type of guy you would've gone out with back in the day just to piss me off."

"If you think Austin is so fucking great, then why would you say he's the kind of guy you'd be pissed to see me with? You can't just pick and choose what works better for you on any given day, Jordan. I know they let you do that when you're on the set. If you want bagels, then they dump all the doughnuts in the trash and get them for you. Real life, the kind the rest of us lives, doesn't work that way."

"I live a very *real life*, thank you very much." Jordan was packing in earnest now. He still wasn't folding any of his clothes or paying much attention to what he was bringing with him, but the bag was filling up quickly. "I think you're the one who needs a reality check."

Annie let out a puff of air, willing to let that one go if she could just make her point. "Jordan, things are different now. You're not just some kid who knows he'll have to take over someday. You *are* the leader of this clan. The very livelihood of everyone in it depends on you. I'm happy to help in any way I can, but it shouldn't feel as though I'm the only one working toward that goal."

"Fine. When I get back from Vegas, I'll sit everyone down and remind them to put the groceries on the marker board. Does that suit you?" He zipped the duffel sharply.

"I think you should quit your acting career. I know you enjoy all the money and fame, but the exposure is too risky for people like us."

Jordan had started to pick up his bag, but now he slammed it back down on the bed. "What? What are you talking about?"

"Everywhere you go, people are trying to take your picture. It's only a matter of time before you do the wrong thing in the wrong place and someone figures out you're a shifter. That'll hurt everyone. You, me, our clan, every other shifter group in the world. It's a huge secret to keep." She pleaded with him with her eyes, mentally begging him to understand.

"Like you'd know anything about keeping that a secret, considering you've never shifted in your life." Jordan snatched the bag and turned for the door.

Annie felt a pit hollow out in her stomach as tears blurred her eyes. She could take the ridicule from anyone else, but not him. Jordan had never insulted her like that, not even when they were kids. She clamped her teeth together, trying to find some response.

"I'm sorry." Jordan dropped the bag once again, this time by the door, and came to sit with her on the bed. "That was a low blow. I shouldn't have said that."

"It's fine," she lied. "Besides, you're just making my point for me."

"What do you mean?"

"I'm not a *real* shifter, and—"

"Yes, you are," he interrupted.

Annie gave him a sharp look, one she'd developed when they were younger and her hardheaded brother wouldn't stop arguing with her just because he was so determined to be right. "No, I'm not. I know there's a bear inside me because I can feel it, but I've never seen it. There's nothing I can do to bring it out. I'm technically in charge when you're gone, but no one respects me. I might as well just be some human servant the rest of you keep around because you feel sorry for me. I can't keep doing this, Jordan."

He was silent for a moment, thinking. Jordan had always been like that. At times, it absolutely infuriated Annie when she felt like he was taking up everyone else's time while he mulled over a situation. He was impulsive in most aspects of his life, so it was difficult for her to understand what made him occasionally decide to slow down.

"I know it's been tough on you not to be able to shift," he finally said. "I saw it as we were growing up, and all the other kids would shift and run off to play in the woods. I know that made you feel left out. But I think there's another side of this situation you could focus on instead."

Annie looked up at him curiously. "What's that?"

"You think you're stuck in your human form, but it just means you have a different way of looking at the world than the rest of us. Don't look at me like that! It's not necessarily a bad thing. Maybe there's a strength to your human side that the rest of us don't see because we're too fixated on our bears. I'm not saying I know what that is, exactly, but I will say you're far more organized and focused."

She rolled her eyes. "Oh, how exciting."

"It's not a bad thing, especially because it means you do such a good job of helping me run this place. I couldn't do it without you, Annie."

"That's all well and good for you to say, but you don't see what it's like when you're gone. If I've got you standing behind me, the rest of the members are willing to listen. As soon as you leave, I might as well be speaking gibberish. You have no idea how little respect they have for me." She could hear the poutiness in her own voice and she hated it, but she was being truthful. The other members didn't seem to care at all about what she said or did, or even that she was the Alpha's sister and technically in charge when Jordan was gone.

He let out a huff of a sigh. "Annie, think about it. If you were so low in their eyes, would someone like Austin be so interested in you? He's a prominent member of our clan, shifts any time he wants to, yet he's never said a single thing about you not being able to. I don't think it matters as much to everyone else as it does to you."

Jordan had a point, and Annie felt it drive home straight to her heart. "Maybe. I'll think on that one. But even if everything you say is true, I think something's going on among our members."

"Like?"

"Most of it is just a feeling, but there are things I notice, too. They stop talking as soon as I walk in the room. Or a few of the men head off and reconvene without saying anything to the rest of us, even when I've got something scheduled for that day." It wasn't anything concrete, but it was something she'd been worried about for a few months. There was a ripple of tension somewhere in the clan, but she couldn't put her finger on it.

"I think you're paranoid."

"I am not! I might not be the Alpha, and I might not be as in touch with my bear as the rest of you are, but that doesn't mean I'm wrong!" Damn it! They'd been heading on a decent track with the conversation, but once again, he had to blow her off. It was always like that with Jordan, and Annie suspected it was because he just didn't want to deal with any problems that might stop him from going to Vegas.

"Okay, okay. I'm sorry. I'll look into it as soon as I get back from my trip, okay? This part of the shoot shouldn't take more than a couple of days, as long as it all goes as planned. Then we can sit down and discuss this in depth. As it is, I'm going to be late for my flight." He patted her on the leg and stood. "You'll do just fine while I'm gone. I promise."

Annie pressed her lips together to stop herself from saying something she might regret. Jordan was good at getting under her skin, but he was still her big brother and she loved him. "Do you need a ride to the airport?"

"Nah. The producer is sending someone to pick me up."

When he'd left, Annie made her way back down to the kitchen. Austin's music was still blaring from the other room, but at least that meant he was busy.

The fridge door shut, revealing a slim woman with her auburn hair pulled up into a ponytail. She smiled at Annie. "Hey! I just updated the grocery list for you. It looks like we're out of pretty much everything."

Annie shrugged. "That's what happens when you live with a bunch of hungry beasts. Here, if you check the fridge and pantry, I'll write everything on the board." She picked up a marker, glad that there was at least one person in the clan who listened to her.

"Definitely meat of all kinds," Michelle said as she peeked into the freezer. "It's like a wasteland in here, and I heard a few of the guys talking about having a barbecue this weekend."

"Of course," Annie muttered under her breath as she scribbled on the board.

"I wouldn't worry about it," Michelle said, immediately picking up on her friend's irritation. "I mean, there are a lot of guys in this clan, and of course they're all bears. They pretty much live to eat."

"I know, but I just had a big conversation with Jordan about how this clan is run and how frustrated I am with all of it. You know, all that stuff we've talked about. I guess I was hoping that if I sat down with him and hashed it all out, he'd finally listen. But no, I'm stuck with everything the same as it's ever been."

"Ice cream," Michelle said as she shut the freezer. "Definitely lots of ice cream. And I know you're frustrated with Jordan, but it could always be worse. We've heard of those other clans where their Alphas and other high-standing members decide to take over territory that doesn't belong to them or use their members for other financial gains. Jordan's arrogant and self-centered, but I don't think he'd let things get too far out of hand."

"You're just saying that because you think he's cute," Annie teased.

Michelle was more than willing to own up to it. "Sure, but I do still think it could be far worse."

"Maybe, I'm just so frustrated. I feel like I'm spinning my wheels, like I used up all my potential when I was young on running around and trying to find new ways to irritate my elders. Now what? I just sit around and make grocery lists and harp at everyone for not picking up their socks? It's not exactly a glamorous life."

"Flour. We're getting a little low on sugar, but I think we're fine for now. Tea. All the good chips are gone." Michelle had her head in the big pantry cabinet, sifting through what was left. She emerged with two bars of dark chocolate and handed one to Annie. "You need this. And a man."

"Not that argument again," Annie said as she rolled her eyes, but she took the candy bar and tore it open. "Jordan was yet again telling me I should go out with Austin."

Michelle had her lips pursed and her eyes raised. "Don't."

"But it could be good for you! You have to admit he's kind of cute, and who wouldn't want to date a musician?"

Annie leaned on the counter. "Someone who prefers peace and quiet."

"I think there's more to it than that," Michelle noted.

"You're right." Annie had been thinking about it a lot, and it was time to say it out loud. After all, Michelle was someone she knew she could trust implicitly. "Austin isn't completely terrible, in the same way that Jordan isn't a completely terrible

Alpha. But you know just as well as I do that I'm supposed to feel something. I'm supposed to get that feeling inside that makes me practically unable to control myself. I don't have that with Austin at all, and I don't know if I ever will. I've never met another shifter who can't shift, so I'm in completely unknown territory. I thought I felt it that one time with Jude, but he obviously didn't feel anything, and it's supposed to be mutual." She tore off another hunk of chocolate, wishing it made her feel better.

"Oh, yeah. That's the guy who used to hang out with your brother, right?"

Jude hadn't been in their clan, he'd only come around to visit now and then. Annie remembered him well; how couldn't she? "Yeah. I swore there was something there. I was so excited because I wasn't sure I'd ever feel it. Jude hardly even looked at me, though, so I must have been mistaken."

Michelle frowned and pulled her close. "Don't get too down on yourself. I think we shifters put way too much pressure on ourselves to find our mates. It's a lot to think about, especially when you consider that the right person for you could be on the other side of the world. And then there's the whole debate on if there's only one person, or if there are more."

Annie sighed, exhausted from so much thinking and feeling. "Yeah, I know. And I know I'm hard on myself. I just feel like I really need to be doing the right thing, especially with Jordan being Alpha."

"I think you're more concerned about it than the rest of us are. Come on. I'll throw some shoes on, and we can go grocery shopping together."

"Thanks." Annie smiled at her friend. There were a lot of things in her life that she'd like to change, but at least she had one person who seemed to understand.

3

Jude refilled his coffee mug and checked the
time. Reid was supposed to call back soon, after he'd
had a chance to discuss a few things with Mali, and
this wasn't the time to be a flake. Sure, his brother
had faced some hard times since leaving the military, and every soldier who suddenly found himself
without the brotherhood of the Army needed time
to adapt. He'd known men who'd roamed the
country without a plan for a full year, just trying to
find something that called to them as much as the
service had. Hell, he'd considered doing that himself
when he'd been honorably discharged. Jude didn't
want to see that happen to Reid. He knew the
Special Ops Shifter Force could be a great home for

him, and he was eager to serve alongside his true blood brother.

His cell vibrated against the counter, and Jude picked it up, expecting to see Reid's number. The top of the screen flashed an indicator saying the call was being imported from his old line, the one he kept before he had an exclusive phone created for the Force by Hudson Taylor in the D.C. unit. It wasn't a number he recognized, but he answered anyway. If it was a telemarketer, then maybe he could have a little fun. "Yeah?"

"Jude?"

The skin along his spine rippled at the sound of her voice. No, that couldn't be right. It'd been years since he'd heard from her, and she had no reason to call him. He cleared his throat. "Uh, yes?"

"It's Annie. Jordan's sister?"

"Hi." He leaned his free hand on the counter, blinking. "It's, um, been a long time."

"I know, and I'm really sorry to bother you. I wasn't even sure if you were stateside right now." Her voice was desperate.

Jude's mind instantly flashed back to one of the last times he'd been around Annie, when he'd come home on leave and visited his best friend, Jordan.

. . .

*J*UDE SAT ON THE SOFA IN THE LIVING ROOM, QUIETLY *relieved to be back in civilization instead of sleeping in a sandy tent. It wouldn't last long, and he'd be back overseas before he knew it, but he'd earned his break. Jordan, his best friend since grade school, seemed more than happy to host him. That is, until his little sister had walked in at midnight.*

"Annie!" Jordan shot up off the couch, his fists curled as he marched toward his sister. "I've been trying to get a hold of you for hours. Where have you been?"

"My phone died, okay?" She was tiny compared to her older brother, all big eyes and waves of dark brown hair. She flashed a look around Jordan at Jude, and her jaw tightened. "I'm fine."

"Were you out with that Dakota guy again?"

Annie tried to move past Jordan to the kitchen, but he wouldn't let her. "What's it to you?"

"The guy's an asshole, that's what."

"Kind of like you're being right now?" She slipped past him through the doorway and glanced once again at Jude. "Sorry to interrupt your visit. I just need to grab my jacket."

"Of course." Moving out of the way so that she could retrieve the garment from the back of the couch, Jude felt something surge inside him. Whatever was happening there was none of his business. As the future

Alpha of his clan, it was up to Jordan to take care of his family. Even so, Jude was overcome with the urge to sweep her up into his arms and fix whatever was bothering her.

"You don't need your jacket," Jordan barked. "It's late, and you need to be in bed. We've got a meeting in the morning."

"I don't care. It's not like anyone cares about what I have to say, anyway." Annie shoved past her brother and left once again, slamming the door behind her.

Jordan plopped back down on the couch and took a swig of his beer. "She kills me, man. I worry about her. This asshole Dakota that she's dating isn't any good for her."

Jude was still staring out the door Annie had gone through, feeling as though his heart had gone through it, too. Annie had always been a pretty girl, but something was different. He grabbed his beer to drench the desert that now occupied his throat. "How old is she now?"

"Eighteen, but that doesn't mean she can just do whatever she wants. The clan comes first, you know?"

Jordan rambled on about responsibility and how important it was for shifters to stick together, but Jude wasn't listening. He was thinking about Annie, and how strange it'd felt to be around her. She wasn't just Jordan's little sister anymore. Never before had she evoked that strange, swirling feeling in Jude's gut that made him want to shift just to get past it.

"...kick the ass of any guy who tries to take advantage of her."

That part caught his attention. "Right. Of course." This was Jordan's younger sister, not just some random hot little piece of ass. That was difficult territory to navigate.

"ARE YOU THERE?"

"Uh, yeah. Sorry. I'm here." He hardly even knew what to say. Why would she suddenly call him after all this time? "How have you been?"

"Not good, actually." Her voice was thick, as though she was trying not to cry. "I know this is a really slim chance, but have you spoken to Jordan lately?"

Jude ran a hand through his hair and then quickly put it back in place, even though she obviously couldn't see him. Hell, his hand was shaking. "Can't say that I have. He seems to be pretty busy now that he's a Hollywood big shot. We've only managed to hang out a couple of times in the last few years."

"Damn. Okay."

"What's going on?" Jude realized Annie wasn't just calling to catch up on old times.

Annie sighed. "Jordan's missing. He was supposed to be back in town after shooting a movie on location. His flight landed yesterday, but he never called to have me pick him up at the airport. Sometimes he just catches a cab or someone from the studio gives him a ride, but I haven't even gotten a text. No one has seen or heard from him, but the rest of the clan thinks I'm just overreacting. I don't know where he is, and I don't know what to do."

"I'll help you." His reply came automatically, without even thinking about it.

A heavy pause sounded over the line, but when Annie spoke again, it was with disbelief. "You will?"

There was no doubt in his mind. "Absolutely." Jude was already grabbing his keys and heading out toward the garage. "I assume you guys are still here in L.A.?"

"Here? You mean, you're in the city, too? I guess I just assumed you were somewhere else, with your military career and everything."

As he started up his sedan and pulled out of the garage, Jude had one thing on his mind, and his inner bear echoed it: *get to Annie as fast as you fucking can.* "I'm actually discharged now, and my current job has me back in the area. I assume you guys still have the same clubhouse?"

"Yep."

"I can be there in about twenty minutes, depending on traffic. I'll be right over." He swung out onto the street, hardly paying attention to the other cars on the road.

"Thanks. Drive safe."

Jude hung up. The logical part of his mind, the one that focused on missions, wondered if he were doing the right thing. After all, Annie hadn't actually asked for help, only if Jude had seen Jordan. He was pulling himself away from any other Force business that might need attention, as well as his brother.

But those gut feelings that he was always trying to tamp down came bubbling to the surface. He'd just been thinking about Annie a few nights ago when he'd been out with Reid. How strange was it for her to be calling him now? Pure coincidence? And that urgency in her voice. It pulled something out from the very center of himself, a place where he'd stuffed so much of his life into the tiniest, densest ball possible to keep it hidden from his day-to-day life.

Jude slammed the steering wheel, frustrated at himself for not being able to look at this logically.

He'd known Annie when she was younger, but when he'd come home on leave and had the chance to visit Jordan, his bear took notice of her in an entirely different way. It didn't mean it was actually that fated pull that he'd been waiting so long for. She was blazing hot, and he was just a young horny guy who hadn't hooked up in a while. There didn't have to be any more to it than that, nor did there have to be any more to their present situation than the fact that she needed help, and he could give it. Jude had one hell of a set of resources at his disposal, after all.

Parking in a side alley, Jude stepped around to the front of the house. Built over a hundred years ago, the Martinez clan house was just as Jude remembered it. A portico jutted out to cover a brick porch. He and Jordan used to climb out the second-story window and hang out on the roof of that portico all the time, dreaming about girls and what they'd do with the rest of their lives. Just to the right was a towering banana tree that took up the entire strip of yard on that side of the walkway.

Jude stepped up to the door, feeling energy move and curl inside his veins as he rang the doorbell. He was just there on business. Helping other shifters was what he did for a living now. If someone called them for help, regardless of whether the Force members knew them or not, they'd help. A nagging voice in the back of his head reminded him that he hadn't even run this past Amar, but he let it go.

Annie answered the door herself, and the second she did, Jude knew he was in trouble. She was no longer a whip of a girl that was his best friend's little sister. Her dark hair and eyes spoke of the Puerto Rican ancestry that Jordan had mentioned at some point. Glazed in a light red, her full lips were in a firm line that said she was all about business, just like the fist on her curved hip.

Somehow, she seemed just as surprised as he did, standing there blinking at him for a moment before she said anything. "That was faster than I expected. Come on in."

Jude followed her into the living room. The furniture had changed since the last time he'd been there, but the house still had the same feeling to it. The thick wood trim and floral wallpaper recalled a time when Hollywood was only in the first stages of being known for the film industry. It was probably old and oppressive to some, but Jude had always found the homeyness of it to be comforting.

"Let's go out here. I don't want to talk inside." Annie led him straight through the house and out the back door, stepping into a gazebo near a large shade tree.

Jude hesitated as he followed her. He felt his bear pounding at the underside of his skin, demanding to claim what he'd been denied for so long. He felt a prickle on the back of his neck as it gained ground, threatening for his other form to come thrusting to the surface. Jude willed the beast back to the best of his ability and sat across from her, as far away as possible without being rude.

"I'm sorry if I jumped the gun on coming out here," he said. "It just sounded like this was a serious situation."

Annie leaned forward and opened a mini-fridge embedded into a serving table in the center of the gazebo. It was hard not to look at her body, studying the luscious way she'd filled out. Even something as simple as the way her dark lashes lay as she looked down into the fridge was driving him absolutely wild. Jude wanted to jump up from his seat and pull her onto his lap. He could easily envision the startled look in those dark chocolate eyes, and his mind quickly changed it to one of intrigue as she let him protect her from whatever the world was throwing at her. No! This was Jordan's sister. There were a million reasons why he couldn't do this. The cold bottle of lemonade she put in his hand only went a short way toward cooling the fire roaring inside him.

"It is a serious situation," Annie said as she sat back down and used her free hand to swipe her thick hair away from her neck against the heat. "It's made all the more serious by the fact that no one around here will listen to me about it."

"Just tell me everything that's happening, and we'll figure it out from there." If he could focus on the details of her crisis, then maybe he could distract himself.

She leaned forward, bracing her elbows on her knees, and took a deep breath. "Jordan was heading to Las Vegas to shoot part of a movie. It was only supposed to take a couple of days. He hasn't come home or called, and he's not answering his phone. I tried talking to the airline to see if he was on his flight, but with all the privacy laws these days, they wouldn't tell me a thing. Same with the hotel where he was staying. I don't have the number of anyone who was involved in the production of the movie." Annie flapped her hands in the air in frustration. "I don't know what else to do."

"It sounds like you've certainly given it a good start. You mentioned that the rest of the clan wasn't worried?"

She made a face he didn't know how to interpret, but the corners of her mouth turned down in disgust. "Everyone thinks I'm just getting upset over nothing. They think Jordan just stayed in Vegas so he could have a little fun. I'm not saying that's impossible, but it's really weird for him to not contact me. Besides, he told me he'd help me out with something when he got back." For a moment, Jude saw a flash of the little girl Annie used to be. The last time he'd seen her, she was an irreverent teenager. But he'd also known her before that, when she was still young and vulnerable.

It made him feel sorry for her, especially since she seemed to be tackling this alone. "Has he done that other times? Stay on location after he's done shooting, I mean."

Annie shook her head. "Most of the time, he doesn't have much of a chance. His career has really taken off, but I'm sure you know that. He's actually at the point of turning down roles because he doesn't have the time."

Jude's mind was working through several ideas, and he was grateful for it. He needed a logical procession of steps to keep himself from wondering if Annie's hair was as soft as it looked. "If you can give me his flight number, I might be able to get the information the airline wouldn't give you. I have a few connections."

Annie closed her eyes as her brows drew together, and when she opened them again, she looked like she was going to cry. "I'd really appreciate that, Jude, but I didn't mean for you to get dragged into this. I was just desperately trying to find some way of getting a hold of Jordan, and I thought of you."

Did she have any idea what she did to him by saying she'd been thinking about him? Blood rushed straight to his groin. "Annie, it's fine. This is actually what I do now."

She tipped her head. "Find missing people? Are you a private investigator or something?"

"In a certain way, I suppose you could say that. I'm actually with the Special Ops Shifter Force." He hadn't asked for clearance to tell her about the Force, and he might pay for that later. They tried to keep themselves as secretive as possible. Like any other shifter, the wrong information with the wrong person could spell serious trouble. Jude knew he could trust Annie, though.

Her head pushed back on her neck. "Seriously? I'd heard rumors about that, but I wasn't sure it was real."

"We're real, all right. All of us served as special ops. We're here specifically for people like you in circumstances like this. I've got some great coworkers who can help us find the information from the hotel and the flight, or even if he rented a car. There's a lot we can do." A reassuring smile spread across his face. "I'm sure we can figure out what's going on."

A tear spilled over her lashes and down onto her cheek. As she rose from the bench and crossed the gazebo, she threw her arms around Jude. "Thank you so much! You have no idea how hard this has been on me, and I've felt so alone."

He instinctively wrapped his arms around her, his bear thrashing inside him at being so close. In that moment, the world could've stopped turning and he wouldn't have noticed. She was sexy as hell, but it was so much more than that. Jude swore he felt her bear responding to his, bonding as two souls that had been split apart when the universe was made and then forced to seek each other out to be reunited once again. He was once again overwhelmed with the urge to carry her away and make everything better, no matter what it took.

When she pulled away to sit next to him, Jude felt cold despite the heat of the day. "I really can't thank you enough for this, Jude. Jordan and I don't always get along, but he's my brother. I'm concerned about him, and I can't help but be worried about what would happen to the clan if he didn't return."

"It'll be all right, Annie." He would make sure of it. He could do a lot more than the average guy, and he'd push himself even further than that if it meant making Annie happy.

"What's going on here?"

Jude turned at the new voice. A man stood at the entrance to the gazebo, his pale blue eyes flicking back and forth between Jude and Annie. The newcomer wore a t-shirt with the sleeves cut off to reveal the tattoos that snaked all up and down his arms, and he didn't look pleased. Jude silently cursed himself for being so caught up in Annie that he hadn't even heard the man approach.

"Austin, this is Jude. He's an old friend of mine. Jude, this is Austin. He's one of our clan members."

Austin extended a hand to shake Jude's, being sure to clamp down with a tight grip. "Nice to meet you."

Jude raised an eyebrow, well aware that he was being challenged. He stopped himself from placing his body between Austin and Annie, knowing that would only escalate things. "You, too."

"Annie, you need any help here?" Austin asked pointedly.

Jude felt his jaw harden. There was clearly something happening between the two of them, and Austin didn't want Jude to be there. Was he hiding something, or was it merely his interest in Annie? Jude knew he had no claim over her. Even if she were feeling the same as he was, she was the sister of an Alpha. She had prominent blood and was second-in-command over this clan. She was also his best friend's sister, and Jude was just an orphan who had nothing to offer her. Still, he was choking on the idea of this Austin character being anywhere near Annie, or even part of the same clan.

"Everything is fine. We're just visiting," Annie replied, her eyes practically shooting lasers at Austin.

His brows lowered and he squared his shoulders, looking ready to fight, but Austin gave her a curt nod. "All right, but I'll be right inside watching. Just yell if you need me." He marched away.

Jude scratched the side of his nose, wondering how he could've forgotten. Annie had always loved bad boys like that douche, the kind who would probably be just as likely to hit her as kiss her. He didn't like it, but he had to remember that this wasn't his territory. "I take it he's your boyfriend?"

Annie's mouth tightened as her eyes widened. "Austin? Not a freaking chance!"

"He certainly seemed interested." Jude once again wrapped a shroud of calm, quiet solitude around himself. Without it, it was too easy to fly off the handle and lose his temper.

She snorted as she stood to retrieve her bottle of lemonade from where she'd left it on the other side of the gazebo. "Oh, sure. He's interested, but I don't think he's *genuinely* interested in me."

Jude kept his gaze on her eyes and the cut of her cheekbones. "Why wouldn't he be?"

Annie didn't seem to notice the implied meaning behind his question. "Austin looks like the kind of guy who wouldn't be interested in anything more than a music career in a metal band, but I think he's power-hungry. Jordan is an Alpha and a Hollywood star, and Austin just wants to kiss his ass. I'm not sure how he thinks that's going to work by doing it through me, but I'm not a psychologist." Her face soured as she glanced toward the house.

Resisting the urge to turn around and see if Austin was watching them through the window, Jude returned the conversation to his original reason for being there. "As far as Jordan goes, email me all the information you have and I'll see what I can find. I may have to fly out to Vegas myself if we don't find any other leads to pursue."

"I'm going with you," Annie said instantly. "If Jordan is out there, I want to be the first person to tell him just how pissed I am at him."

The two of them flying off to Vegas together? Once again, Jude felt his body and his mind wandering to places where they didn't belong. "We don't know what's really going on. It could be dangerous."

"I don't care. Jude, I've been spending too long sitting here worrying about everything. Jordan himself called me out for being too invested in the day-to-day running of the house instead of thinking on a bigger scale. I don't want to admit it, but he's right. I need to get out a little more, and I'm plenty capable." She paced back and forth as she spoke, flinging her hands through the air as though she were casting aside any doubts that Jordan or the others had about her.

Jude nodded. "All right. Give me a day to see what I can come up with, and then I'll call you." He stood and turned to go, ready to get out of there. There were too many uncertainties. Could he really believe Annie when she said she wasn't involved with Austin? If Austin was interested in her only as a means to finding power, then why was he so suspicious of Jude? Could it be at all possible that Annie might care for him the same way he cared for her? It would be much easier if he could distance himself from her and focus on the intelligence aspect of finding Jordan.

"Jude." She said his name as he stepped out of the gazebo onto the grass.

Her voice sent a shudder of excitement through his body, and he reminded his bear that he only wanted her because he couldn't have her. "Yeah?"

"Thank you."

He turned to see genuine appreciation in her eyes, and it cut straight to his heart. He'd seen that look before, when he'd served overseas and had helped liberate towns from oppressive leaders. That was the look of the people who needed help, the ones who needed it so badly, they'd do almost anything to get it. Many times, Jude never knew what ended up happening to those people he'd helped. He hoped he'd get to know the rest of Annie's story, at least. "No problem."

He headed back to the house, dialing Raul's number on the way.

4

———

"LADIES AND GENTLEMEN, PLEASE FASTEN YOUR seatbelts and put up your trays as we prepare for landing at McCarran International Airport in Las Vegas."

Annie did as the flight attendant asked, feeling cramped and stiff despite the short flight from L.A. Jude had argued a second time against her coming with him to search for Jordan, but she'd insisted. To Annie, any amount of danger and intrigue didn't matter to her. She just wanted to find her brother, chew him up one side and down the other for making her worry, and get back home.

Now that they were actually on their way, she was starting to regret it. Though she'd sat next to Jude during the flight, her body surging toward him the entire time, he'd hardly said a word. She'd tried to start conversations with him about the weather or the view, and they always fizzled out after a few exchanges.

It was incredibly frustrating. Annie hadn't expected to feel what she did for Jude when he showed up at her home. When she'd opened the door, she was shocked to find every cell of her body reacting to his presence. He was older now, and he'd matured into a gorgeous, hard-bodied soldier. With his pale brown hair hanging over his forehead and those mesmerizing green eyes, she'd wanted to throw herself over the threshold at him.

He'd come on business, though. He'd come to help his childhood best friend. If the way Jude was acting was anything to go by, Annie didn't have anything to do with it.

She stood and stretched as they waited for their turn to deboard, watching the back of Jude's neck. His brawny frame towered over her, and Annie couldn't help but wonder if other women on the flight had noticed him. The flight attendant who'd smiled so sweetly at him when she'd brought his crackers and a tiny cup of soda had certainly let her gaze linger for a little too long.

"So, what's the plan?" Annie asked as they

filtered through the airport toward the luggage carousel. "You said Jordan wasn't on his flight or in his hotel, and you were able to find out that he hadn't rented a car anywhere, but is there anything you did find?"

He glanced at her before quickly reverting his gaze to the spinning rack of suitcases, reaching forward to snag both his and hers in one quick movement. "We really shouldn't talk about it here."

Annie tightened her lips. He didn't seem to want to talk at all, which was going to make this a very long trip, no matter how quickly they were able to find Jordan. "I understand, but it's not like anyone else here is paying attention to us." The airport was busy as passengers darted back and forth to catch their planes or move on to their final destinations, and no one had even given them a second glance.

Jude gave her that look again. "Annie, I realize it might look that way. We need to be as cautious as possible. Let's get settled into our hotel and get a feel for the area. Then we'll talk."

"Fine." Annie kept her mouth clamped tightly shut as she and Jude caught a cab from the airport, thinking about the situation she'd gotten herself into. First, she was in a horrible position with the rest of the clan. Austin had questioned her thoroughly when she'd explained she was leaving, and something had kept Annie from telling him that she was taking a trip with Jude. Annie had never thought she'd be the kind of person who'd lie to her clan members. After all, her job and her life were all about taking care of them. But given the way Austin had reacted to Jude's presence when he'd come to the house, and that no one but her seemed interested in finding out why Jordan hadn't come home, Annie made up a story about visiting a friend who wasn't doing well. Austin had been left in charge, believing she was in Oregon.

Then, there was the problem with Jude. She'd called him in a desperate attempt to see if he'd heard from Jordan, and then he'd shown up. Annie hadn't expected that. Now she was stuck working alongside a man she could hardly resist, and it was making her angry. She was mad at herself for feeling this way about him, and frustrated with him for obviously not wanting to have anything to do with her. Hell, Jude hadn't even wanted her to go to Vegas to search for her own brother. Once again, Annie was just the tagalong that no one wanted.

She squinted out the window at the brilliant sunshine that illuminated the hotels, restaurants, and 24-hour wedding chapels that dotted the city. It might have been a decent place for some folks to visit, but right now, she just wished everything was back to normal.

The cab pulled up in front of the Bellagio, and Annie tried not to look astonished as she got out of the vehicle and gazed up at the tall building while the fountains erupted behind her. She'd known that Vegas would be glamorous, and her brother's career gave him the chance to stay at all sorts of impressive places, but Annie had never been to any of them with him. "This is where he was staying?"

"That's what my sources tell me," Jude replied with his usual solemn manner as he pulled their suitcases out of the trunk and nodded toward the revolving doors.

Annie didn't want him to know just how overwhelmed she was as she took in the expansive lobby with its marble floor and art glass fixed to the ceiling. Every single thing, from the door handles to the light fixtures to the little sign in a flower bed, looked to be top-of-the-line. It made Annie realize just what a sheltered life she'd been living, and it bothered her. If her brother was a big star, and if she was second-in-command of a Hollywood clan, then why did she live such a simple life? It was yet another way that she was different from everyone else around her, and it only made her more irritable as she waited for Jude to check in for them.

The elevator ride to their floor was just as silent as their flight had been. Annie folded her arms in front of her chest, wondering just how long she could handle it. She opened her mouth to ask him what she'd done to anger him when the elevator dinged and let them off on their floor.

"Here's your room," Jude said as he handed her a keycard. "I'm right here, and there's a door adjoining the two. I thought that would be the safest option, just in case." His mouth twitched slightly as he turned on his heel and went to his room. He paused at his door without looking back at her. "Let's take an hour to settle in, and then we can get started."

The luxury that waited for Annie on the other side of the door was fabulous, but she hardly cared as she flopped down on the bed and pulled her cell out of her pocket to call Michelle.

"Hey! How was your flight?"

"Tense, just like everything else." Annie had told Michelle the truth about her trip, and it was nice to have someone to vent to. "I must have done some-thing wrong, but I have no idea what. Jude will barely talk to me. He hardly even looks at me! And I'm not even worried about it being in a romantic way at this point. It's just so obvious that he's avoiding me."

"Don't overanalyze it. Some people don't travel well. From the tone of your voice, it sounds like you're one of them."

Annie scowled at the ceiling. "Maybe, but everything seemed fine when he came to the house. Something changed, and I can't help but wonder if Jordan told him at some point that I can't shift."

Michelle sighed. "Even if he did, it's not like Jude is going to hate you for that. And Jordan would have to have told him a long time ago, since you don't know where he is right now. Just calm down and at least try to enjoy yourself while you're there."

"Easier said than done." Annie's next scowl was directed at the door that joined their two rooms. "It's going to be really awkward."

"What if Jude just doesn't know how to act because he's never had a civilian on a mission with him?" Michelle suggested.

It was reasonable. In fact, it made far more sense than any of the wild thoughts that'd been zinging through Annie's mind. Her body was out of control, craving him, wishing she could do something spontaneous like throw her arms around him the way she had in the gazebo again. Annie's father had always said the most reasonable explanation was usually the right one. "Yeah. You could be right. How's everything going at the house?"

"Oh, fine. Austin is taking advantage of the fact that you put him in charge, but only with dumb guy stuff like starting a poker tournament or a pool party. Harmless, really."

"He doesn't have any access to the finances or anything, so there's only so much he can do." Annie frowned, wishing she'd had a better choice than Austin. Michelle certainly would've been a good one, but she didn't rank high enough to be put in charge without others throwing a fit. "Just take care, and make sure you let me know if you run into any trouble."

"Of course."

After hanging up, Annie pushed herself off the bed and forced herself to unpack, take a shower, and get dressed. She felt a little better, trying to remind herself that it didn't matter if she liked Jude or not. She could be professional, as he was. This wasn't about her or him or anything else. It was about Jordan. Still, she stood in front of the big mirror in the bathroom, trying to decide which shirt she should wear. Something black with a little glitz of sequins at the bottom? Something more casual? The sun was falling quickly, but Annie had no idea what the rest of the evening held for her.

She was forced to make a decision when Jude knocked on the door between their rooms.

"Damn it," she muttered as she threw on the black shirt and crossed the room to let him in.

He didn't actually have to duck to get through the door, but the way he carried his head made it seem as though he had. Why did he have to be so goddamn irresistible? Why did she have the urge to press her head against his chest and listen to his heartbeat? Annie could feel her bear protesting beneath the surface of her skin, angry and frustrated at its continued denial of freedom. She shook it off, reminding herself that she'd already decided to be professional, but it wasn't working very well.

This was only made harder by the fact that Jude had dressed in fitted jeans that hugged his ass just right. He'd paired them with a pale green button-down which enhanced the color of his eyes.

His eyes swept down her body and quickly snapped back up to her face. "I hope I gave you enough time."

She put a hand to her face, worried for a moment that she'd forgotten to put on makeup or brush her hair. Annie realized she was just thinking too hard about a simple statement yet again. "Yeah. Of course. I wasn't sure what to wear since I didn't know what we were doing."

His mouth twitched in the closest thing she'd seen resembling a smile since they'd left L.A. "It's perfectly fine. I'd like to get a feel for the area and just spend some time here before making too many inquiries about Jordan."

Annie frowned. "Isn't that a waste of time? I thought we'd be sneaking into the kitchens or questioning the staff." As soon as she said it, Annie realized how dumb that sounded. This wasn't a movie, and Jude was supposed to know what he was doing.

"You can keep any torture devices you brought along stowed away for the moment," he said, humor in his voice. "I know it sounds like a waste, but I'm thinking of this whole city as enemy territory right now. There's plenty of recon I can do in terms of satellite images and databases, but it's important to know the feel of a place, too. If you're paying attention, you can get a feel for what illicit things might happen in a place that seems completely tame."

"Oh." Annie turned away from him and busied herself with taking her shoes out of the closet. "I didn't know that. I guess that means you think something bad really did happen to Jordan?"

"I'm trying not to speculate and just go with facts. All records of him fizzle out shortly after he checked out of the hotel. Annie?"

She was still kneeling in front of the closet, trying to keep the tears that burned the backs of her eyes from spilling down her cheeks. "It's fine. I'm fine. I'm sorry. I just got a little emotional there for a second."

His hand was so warm as his palm smoothed across her shoulder, she thought it might burn her up from the inside out. "This is why I wasn't sure about you coming along with me."

"Are you sure?" she retorted, shaking off his hand and standing. "I figured it was just because you didn't want Jordan's annoying little sister dogging your footsteps and getting in the way."

"Hey." She'd tried to step away from him, but his grip was firm as he pulled her close and bent his head to look her in the eyes. "It's not like that at all. You have to remember that I've been in this business for a long time now. I know how difficult it is for someone to get involved when they think the life of their loved one might be at stake. This isn't going to be easy. I can tell you've got a lot of fire in you. If you think you can use it, then come with me. If you don't think you're up for it, then stay here, relax, get a massage if you want to, and know that I have this handled."

All of her breath left her body. Jude was standing in front of her, promising to take care of her. His words had turned into a lightning bolt that struck her right in the center of her heart. Instead of killing her, it brought her to life and sent a tingling sensation through her core, radiating out to her limbs.

It was only that tiny nagging thought of Jordan that brought her back to reality. "I'll come with you," she finally said, her throat dry. "I want to be involved in this, and I'd like to think I can be."

"Just promise me that if at any point it doesn't work out for you, you'll come back here. I can even arrange security for you if need be. I just don't want anything to happen to you, Annie." His soft eyes lingered on her face for a long moment before he strode to the window. "There's a lot in this city, and the heavy tourism is going to make it a little harder. I've got someone working with advanced facial recognition technology that can be applied to almost all the cameras in the city. That, I think, is going to be our easiest route, but while we wait, we just need to do as much observation as possible."

"Okay." He made it all sound so easy. "I'm not sure how two people are supposed to do that.

There are hundreds of thousands of people living here, not to mention the millions of tourists." Annie had done a bit of research before she'd left, but it hadn't truly prepared her for what she was getting into.

"Just trust that I have this as well covered as possible. It might feel like it's only the two of us, but it isn't. Do you trust me, Annie?"

Damn those eyes! Jude could be asking her to believe the moon was made of cheese and she'd have to say yes. She really did trust him, though. There were so few people in the world who believed in her, and Jude seemed to be one of them. "Yes."

"Good. Then let's get started."

A short time later, they were across the street, surging upward in a glass-walled elevator. Despite herself, Annie felt a smile playing across her lips.

"What is it?"

"What?" The small crowd of people meant the two of them were crushed together in the small space. Annie was aware enough of Jude even when they were in an open space, but now she could feel the heat that radiated from his body. His scent invaded her senses, making her wonder what it would feel like to run her hands over the smooth planes of his bare chest.

"That big smile on your face," he said, his breath tickling her ear.

She lifted one shoulder and let it fall. "When we decided to take this trip, I thought it would be a little different than this. I knew this replica of the Eiffel Tower was here, but I didn't think we'd be going up in it."

He glanced through the glass at the structure that passed by as they rose ever higher. "Things aren't always what we expect."

Annie had the distinct feeling that he was talking about much more than this tourist trap. She felt him put his hand on her lower back as they stepped out of the elevator at the top and reminded herself that Jude was just being a gentleman. When they found Jordan, he'd want to know that Annie was safe and taken care of, after all.

They stepped out onto the viewing platform. The railing was caged all around to keep tourists from doing anything stupid, but even before they stepped up to it, Annie could feel the warm breeze washing through her hair. A couple in the corner stood with their cheeks pressed together as they looked out over the city. Nearby, a man was down on one knee with a ring box in his hand and a hopeful look on his face as he gazed up at the woman he wanted to marry.

Jude cleared his throat uncomfortably as he guided Annie around to the other side of the tower. The sun was sinking quickly behind the mountains in the distance, creating a deep blue bowl overhead that capped the lights of Vegas as they glowed to life. The fountains in front of their hotel flipped and thrashed as they went through their routine.

Annie curled her fingers around the grate, glad it was there.

"I know it doesn't seem like much in the way of our mission," Jude said, his body pressed close to hers as they kept as far away from the rest of the visitors as possible. "It's just one of those gut things."

"And what does your gut tell you about Jordan?" She almost didn't want to ask. It was too easy to get lost in the romance of their location. This was where people went to do the things they couldn't bring themselves to do in their regular lives, whether it was gambling or getting married or even just relaxing. If she let it, this could be her chance to show Jordan and everyone else in the clan that she was more than capable of being a leader. That was more important than anything, so why did she yearn for him to throw her over his shoulder and carry her back to his room?

"That he's all right, but that he needs our help," he replied quietly. "Jordan and I haven't had a lot of time together over the last few years. We've both been very busy, but I know what sort of guy he is. He can get lost in things like show business, just like anyone else could, but he's got a good head on his shoulders and good instincts. I don't think he'd get himself into any trouble on purpose."

Annie's face pinched as she thought about her brother. "What kind of trouble do you think he's in?"

"There are too many questions and far too few answers," he said cryptically.

She could agree with that, though, not just about Jordan, but about herself and even Jude. "And it seems we only keep finding those questions."

"That's not surprising. It's going to feel that way until this is all over with." He smiled at her when she looked up at him in confusion. "You get used to it eventually. You hungry?"

Coming back down the Eiffel Tower and moving through the strip, the crowds pressed in close around them. Everything was brilliant lights and signs and people shouting, and Annie felt over-whelmed by the crush of it all. She narrowed her focus on the center of Jude's muscular back as he threaded through the tourists, but there was too much to see. She was constantly craning her head to see the lights or one of the many street performers. A man posed as a statue in various positions, and another dressed as Elvis created quick spray paint art on small canvases that he pawned to passersby. Several superhero characters promised a photo for a few bucks, and musicians and magicians were dotted along between them. Annie paused to watch one of them pull card after card out of a rabbit's ear when she felt a warm hand slip into hers. She started to jerk it away when she realized it was Jude.

"I thought I lost you for a minute," he said, sincerity radiating from his eyes.

"Sorry. I just got distracted."

"That's all right. We're going to have to cut our little recon mission short, anyway. I just got word that someone matching Jordan's description was seen out on the west edge of town." Jude tugged on her hand as they headed back to their hotel.

She fell into step beside him, not sure if she should feel hopeful, angry, or elated.

5

———

Jude tensed his hands on the wheel of their rental car. "Aren't you going to eat that?" he asked, nodding his head toward the In-N-Out Burger bag in her lap.

"I don't know that I can. I'm too nervous." Annie bit her lip. Her arms were folded over her chest as she looked out the window.

He could understand that. When he'd gotten the call from his Force comrade, Raul, Jude had hardly wanted to believe it. Why would Jordan not only suddenly refuse to come home, but settle down in a rental out on the edge of town? If Jordan were going to settle down in Vegas, he'd want someplace right in the middle of the downtown hubbub. He was just that kind of guy, or else he'd never have made it as an actor.

Jude was also concerned about having Annie with him. God, it'd been nearly impossible to control himself already, and they'd hardly even started! The plane ride had been excruciating, feeling her right there next to him. He'd booked their hotel rooms right next to each other for safety's sake, but he also knew that meant she was right next door. Even as he'd stowed away his suitcase and heard the water running in his suite, he'd imagined the soapy lather sliding over her breasts and down her thighs. It was the kind of thing a teenage boy should be fantasizing about, not him.

And then there'd been that ridiculous trip to the top of the Eiffel Tower. Jude hadn't been lying when he'd told her it was the beginning of their surveillance to help them get a feel for the area. He really did want to see it all in one big view. It was just like climbing a tree or heading up to the roof of a building to see the lay of the land and how people flowed through it. But he also found himself wanting to be in a place like that with a woman like her. No, not *like* her. Her. Just Annie.

Did she have any idea what she did to his bear?

He'd seen the fire and passion in her eyes when she'd insisted on coming on this trip. Some of it, he knew, was some sort of desperation to prove something. Some of it was likely out of concern for her brother. At its heart, though, Jude knew that Annie was more than most people could see. She wasn't just the head of a clan who worried for her members. Still, all of her fine qualities might not mean squat if they ended up having to actually face an enemy. Jude had to keep her safe for Jordan's sake. He could only hope that their lead brought them straight to the man, and then it would all be over. Jude could wash his hands of the whole situation and go on pretending there was nothing between the two of them.

"All right," he said as they pulled up in front of a house in a very modern, angular design that seemed to be popular in the area. "I don't have a whole lot of information. I only know that he was seen here. He might be here, he might not. I don't know if anyone else is inside, so basically, we have to be ready to fight."

"Fight? It's my brother," Annie reasoned. "If he's gone off on some bender or is having an early midlife crisis, it's not like I'm going to hogtie him and throw him in the trunk. I just want to know that he's okay."

Jude pinched the bridge of his nose. Annie was a smart girl, but that was her problem. She was trying to be reasonable in a situation that might not be reasonable at all. "You work with shifters every day. You know that our animal sides keep us from doing things the same way normal humans would. All I'm saying is that we have to be prepared for the worst."

She shot him that look again, the one that said she didn't like being told what to do, but she nodded. "All right."

It didn't make Jude feel any better as he stepped out of the car and walked up to the door. His eyes roved over every aspect of the building he could see, wanting to be one step ahead of any ambush that might happen. It all seemed quiet as he walked onto the porch and knocked on the door.

The man who answered looked remarkably like Jordan. He had the same dark, wavy hair, steely blue eyes, and square jaw that had become so famous on the silver screen. Even though it'd been a while since Jude had seen Jordan, though, he knew this wasn't him.

Annie had noticed as well. "You're not my brother," she accused.

The man looked back and forth between them before he stepped back and swung the door shut.

Jude's hand shot out, crunching against the wood to stop him, and he shoved harder, pushing it open.

"Shit!" The man let go of the door and darted toward the back of the house.

Jude instantly went after him. He was in his human form on the outside, but his bear instincts had taken over. He barreled into the house, hearing the door slam back and shiver on its hinges. The man knocked a lamp off an end table, but Jude easily cleared it as he charged into the kitchen. The back door was just within reach, but the man who wasn't Jordan had locked it. He was fiddling with the latch when Jude snagged him by the back of the shirt and yanked him backward. Not-Jordan flung his arms out to catch himself, landing a glancing blow to Jude's jaw. He was trying to pull Jude down to the floor with him when Annie stormed up and stomped her heel into the man's crotch.

"Ah!" Not-Jordan squeaked, immediately stopping any efforts to get away or gain an advantage. "What the fuck! You didn't have to do that!"

"You didn't have to run away," she pointed out.

Jude gave her a quick, appraising look before pointing at an extension cord hanging near the garage door. "Hand me that." It didn't take long to tie him up in a chair while Annie went back into the living room to shut the front door.

Pulling a chair up so that he sat in front of the man, Jude took a moment to calm himself. Adrenaline was still pumping through his system, and his body was fighting him as to what form he should be in. His bear wanted to come out and swat this asshole around a little, but Jude knew that he needed to be calm and collected.

"Who the fuck are you?" Clearly, Annie didn't feel the same way. She was bent forward, her face only an inch from their captive's. "Obviously, something's going on here, or you wouldn't have tried to bolt like that."

The man curled away from her, probably not wanting to get his package smashed a second time. "Hey, I don't know who you two are or what you're doing here. What do you expect me to do?"

"Annie." Jude pressed his tongue against his teeth, waiting for her to turn around and look at him. She didn't, but she did back off. She came to stand next to Jude, one hand on her hip and one foot tapping impatiently against the cheap linoleum.

Jude leaned forward. "Now that you're finally willing to listen to us, I'll tell you that we're here looking for Jordan Martinez. I find it odd that you look so much like him."

"Yeah, well, I'm his stunt double, Evan Boyer. But I haven't seen Jordan for a couple of days."

"You sure went down quickly for a stunt man," Annie commented.

"That's because they don't try to demolish my dick when I'm on set," Evan replied with a sneer.

"I'm sorry about that," Jude replied, not giving Annie a chance. He had a good feeling she wasn't sorry at all, but they needed to get any information they could out of this guy. "We might've gotten a little carried away. We're here because Jordan hasn't been seen or heard from in the last several days. We were notified that someone fitting his description was seen here, and it turns out to be you. Perhaps you have some insight as to where Jordan is."

A bead of sweat stood out on Evan's face. "What are you, the police or something?"

Jude smiled. "Something like that."

"Well, I don't have to say anything. I don't know who you are or what you want, or why the hell you think I have anything to do with it. I suggest you untie me right now unless you want to find your asses in jail. I have a lot of connections, you know!" Evan struggled against the extension cord.

Annie jumped forward, ready to go at him again, but Jude grabbed her by the waist and held her back. She struggled against him, her backside twisting and turning against his front, and damn it if he didn't like it. He smiled at Evan over her shoulder. "Talk, or I let her do what she wants. I don't have to tell you she's a little pissed right now."

She was either playing into the scene or was genuinely angry, but Annie lurched forward to swing at Evan, just missing his face.

"Fine! Fine! Jesus, nothing scarier than a crazy bitch."

"I'll fucking gut you if you speak to her that way again," Jude warned.

"God! All right. Sorry." Evan glanced at the back door, probably wondering if he had any chance of escaping, then deciding he didn't.

Jude held onto Annie with just one arm now, not quite trusting her enough to let her go completely. She wasn't being rational, and he couldn't blame her, but he didn't want to squander this opportunity. "Tell me about the last time you saw Jordan."

"I was out here to shoot a few scenes for the movie. It was an action film, so of course, there were plenty of shots for his stunt double. They've been hiring me for every flick he does because I look so much like him. It's great that I get steady work, but it sucks for him to get all the glory, you know?"

"Go on."

Evan glanced up at Annie again, who had calmed down with Jude's arm around her. "You sure you've got her?"

He could feel her vibrating in his arms, ready to attack. Jude smiled. "For the moment. You might want to hurry up."

"Okay. Well." Evan swallowed. "I figured that if something tragic happened to Jordan, like he got in a car accident or fell off a cliff or something, I could pretty easily slip in to take over his career. They'd ask me to finish shooting the movie in his place since we're practically twins, and it would spin off from there. They'd have the looks *and* the stunt man all rolled into one."

"You murdered my brother?" Annie screeched, struggling toward Evan once again. "I'm going to kill you!"

"No! I didn't!"

Jude stood, put both his arms around her, and swung her to the side. "Keep it up," he whispered in her ear. This was working. He pretended to legitimately struggle against keeping Annie in check, and even though she was much stronger than she looked, he had a good handle on her.

"I didn't kill him! I was going to, but I didn't get the chance! I told him we'd go out for some beers and a night on the town when we were done shooting, and I slipped him a few pills. He passed out just like I planned, but when he woke up, he turned into a bear! It scared the fuck out of me, but I still had him tied up. I thought maybe I could use him in a completely different way and make a shit ton of money off blackmail or selling him to some freak show, but these other guys showed up and paid me for him."

"Who?" Jude demanded.

"I don't know. They didn't even use their first names, but they didn't seem surprised at all that the dude had turned into a fucking bear. It was the weirdest thing, but it was easy money and I wasn't going to turn it down."

"Where did they take him?"

"I don't know. They didn't tell me a thing. They just handed me a bag of cash, loaded Jordan up like some circus animal, and left."

Annie was fighting against Jude in earnest now, truly ready to rip this man to shreds. "I suggest you tell me everything you know," Jude warned.

"It was a big blonde guy in a black Jeep. A pretty new one. That's all I know. Jesus Christ, she's going to kill me!"

Annie had managed to slip Jude's grip slightly, snarling as she lunged toward Evan.

"Not if I can help it!" boomed a loud voice from the kitchen doorway.

All three of them turned to see a large man. His head was shaved, and his muscles rippled under his fitted t-shirt as he came into the room. "What the fuck is going on here? Evan, is this some twisted sex game or something?"

"Keith! Thank God! These crazy fuckers broke in and tied me up! I think they were trying to rob us." Evan wriggled in his chair, making it thump against the floor.

"I don't think so." Keith moved into the room and reached forward with one meaty hand to wrap it around Jude's neck.

Jude smiled at the mountain of a man. Evan was lying, but Jude had an advantage. He let his human form fall away, and by the time Keith grabbed him, he was clutching the throat of a bear.

"What the fuck?" Keith scrambled back to reveal another man who'd come in. This one wasn't as big as Keith, but the way he dodged out of the way made Jude think he was yet another stunt double. Great.

"They're some sort of bear freaks! Just like Jordan!" Evan screeched. He was bouncing in earnest in his chair now, trying to get to the door.

Jude let go of Annie. She went after Evan, issuing a swift kick to his chest that sent him sprawling backward on the floor. She darted past Keith and slammed her fist into the jaw of the second man.

Focusing on Keith, Jude rushed forward on four legs. His roar filled the room and echoed off the ceiling as his teeth clamped down on the big man's arm. He tasted of salt and grime, but Jude didn't let that stop him. He bit down hard, yanking his head to the side to increase the size of the wound. Blood filled Jude's mouth as Keith's scream overtook his own. A yank brought him down to the floor. Jude's claws sank into his flesh as he trampled him to get to Annie.

She'd made the other man bleed profusely from his nose, but he'd managed to get his hand into her hair. He yanked her head backward. "You stupid little bitch!" he screamed, pulling his fist back as he prepared to land a punch.

Jude was already possessed with the spirit of his bear, but his sight went red with rage. Nothing could stop him as he slammed his body into the other man's. Annie's hair fell from his hands as Jude ripped into his torso, keeping his promise. The body went limp beneath his paws, but Jude didn't care. Something even deeper than his inner animal had been activated, the part of him that wanted to protect Annie at all costs. He'd gone completely wild.

"Jude! Jude!" Her hand was on his shoulder.

He pulled back, seeing just what he'd done. Jude turned away as he shifted, lumbering back into the kitchen as he slowly morphed into walking upright once again. He turned on the kitchen faucet, washing his hands and splashing his face. "Are you all right?" he asked hoarsely.

"Yeah, I'm fine. Just a little banged up, but I'll be okay. What about you?"

Drying his hands on his jeans, he turned to look at Annie. The skin around her eye was discolored. "You're going to have a shiner."

"Whatever. What do we do about *them*?" She gestured with her head to the two remaining men.

"Nothing. Come on." He took her by the arm as they went out the front door and into the night air. It felt too cold on his bare skin. "They were in on it with Evan. From what he said, they knew about

Jordan. I'll call in what information I have to my headquarters so the search can continue. For now, this is a dead end."

Annie was quiet as they headed back toward downtown. She combed her fingers through her tangled hair and fidgeted uncomfortably in her seat, tucking her hands between her knees and then against her sides. She said nothing.

"I know it probably doesn't seem like it, but that was a start toward finding Jordan. I'll get the vehicle tracked down, and we'll find him."

"Okay," was her only response.

He wasn't good at this. He'd turned into something completely undomesticated back there, a bear who had no sense of morality or when to stop. "If you're bothered that I killed that guy, just know that he deserved it. He was going to kill us if he had the chance."

"It's fine."

Jude was on autopilot as he drove, paying almost no attention to traffic or signs, but knowing he was heading in the right direction. He wanted to make this better for Annie. "You know, you were pretty savage back there. I'm impressed at how well you did against those assholes."

"I did grow up with a brother and all the other

guys in our clan," she reminded him quietly. "Things were usually a little wild."

"Yeah. I guess that's true." Jude hadn't thought of that. He and Reid had wrestled plenty of times, and even though the Hoffmans' had brought them into their clan, it wasn't the same. "You're pretty lucky."

She didn't respond.

He was messing this up completely. Jude wanted to help. He'd run to her rescue without even talking to Amar. The rest of the Force was well aware of the situation and helping him out remotely, but maybe it would've been better if he'd asked Gabe or Raul to go in his place. They would've been far more impartial, and they wouldn't have felt obligated to bring Annie along. "Look, I know you're upset. Whether it's because you're worried about Jordan or that you're upset with me, we can talk about it. I know you can't be happy. You didn't even shift during that fight back there."

Annie turned to him, the streetlights flashing intermittently on her face. She opened her mouth to speak and slammed it shut again, turning away toward the passenger window.

Jude's teeth gritted together so hard it made his jaw hurt, but he didn't care. Annie was in emotional pain, worried her brother would never come home again. Maybe she was pissed at Jude for his violence, but that wasn't something he could get around. He'd killed before—both in combat and while serving with the Force—and he'd probably have to do it again.

He was infatuated with a woman who could never possibly love him back. She had the clan life and a sense of belonging that he would never understand, and Jordan—wherever he was—would kill him in an instant if he acted on what he felt. He'd put himself in a completely impossible situation.

She was still quiet as they went up to their rooms. Jude hesitated in the hall just long enough to hear her bolt the door behind her before he went into his own, wanting to make sure she was safe. He showered, letting the hot water wash over him in the hopes that it could rinse away all his feelings, but it only made things worse.

With a towel wrapped around his waist, he made sure the door that joined their rooms was unlocked. He couldn't keep fantasizing that she might suddenly come to him, revealing that she, too, had been turned on as he'd held her back in Evan's kitchen.

That she felt all the same turmoil inside that he'd been suffering from.

That she knew she wanted to be with him forever.

That they'd been cut from the same cloth when the universe had whirled to life.

He just wanted her to be safe. That was his duty at this point, no matter what had happened to Jordan.

He dialed Raul. "Apparently, the facial recognition software doesn't account for stunt doubles."

"*Mierda.* Are you serious?"

Jude swiped a hand down his face, still feeling tired and dirty even though he'd showered. "Yeah. Things have only gotten more complicated. I've got a vehicle you can look for, though. It'll be a pain since I don't have a plate number, but it was at that same house within the past week."

"I can do it," the wolf promised.

"I know. I'm just not sure I can."

Raul let out a snort. "You've gotten yourself in over your head with this girl, haven't you?"

"Is it that obvious?" Jude rolled his eyes toward that damn shared door once again.

"I knew it had to be something big if it could pull you away from L.A. right as your brother got into town."

Shit. He'd hardly spared a thought for Reid ever since Annie had called. "Is everything all right?"

"Oh, sure. We've just been spending some time with him, letting him know how we do things. There isn't much happening down here at the moment, so that makes it a little easier. Don't worry about any of it."

"Thanks. Let me know as soon as you find out about this Jeep. We'll follow it. If we haven't heard anything from you by the morning, we'll just head back to L.A. It's probably a good idea to get Annie back home."

"Sounds good."

They hung up, and Jude went to the window of his room. There was a certain kind of beauty in the hectic energy of the city, though he usually preferred more rural settings. Even so, it was hard to appreciate it when he knew Annie was so upset with him.

6

ANNIE STOOD RIGHT IN FRONT OF THE DOOR THAT LED to Jude's room. She reached for the knob, but then she dropped her hand before she managed to turn it. Instead, she tried to explore the hotel room. It was luxurious and by far the most beautiful place she'd ever stayed. It should have been exciting, but there was too much on her mind for her to enjoy it.

Where was Jordan? Was he still out there somewhere in Vegas? Who had come to literally buy him from Evan? It was the most convoluted thing she could've fathomed. What if it was someone from the government? What would this mean for their clan and the rest of the shifters in the world?

She sank down on the bed and braced her forehead on her palm, staring at her phone and trying to decide if she should call Michelle or not. Annie needed someone to talk to. She had to get some of this off her mind, but no one could give her answers. Even Jude could only do so much, and he'd assured her he would find Jordan.

Jude. Annie glanced up at that door once more, knowing he was just on the other side of it. She'd been horribly rude to him. He'd misread her, thinking she was angry with him.

She pressed her lips together as she thought. *Does he deserve to know the truth? Would he even care?* She felt so much for him, and yet it was obvious those feelings weren't mutual. He was putting himself in harm's way to help her, though. The least she owed him was an explanation.

The day had been long enough, but Annie summoned the last ounce of courage she had in her body and stood. She knocked on the door.

He answered so quickly, the breeze from opening the door played with his wet hair. His eyes were wide, his lips slightly parted, and his chest incredibly bare. He wore nothing but a pair of athletic shorts, which showed the impressive muscle he'd built during his time in the service. A fine dusting of hair graced his chest, growing thicker as it trailed toward the waistband of his shorts. She knew she shouldn't look at him this way, but she couldn't help it.

"Is everything all right?" he asked.

"Um, yeah. I just wanted to talk to you for a minute."

He stood there for the longest second in all eternity before he stepped back and held the door open wide. "Come in."

His room was a mirror image of hers, and it shouldn't have embarrassed her to see the large bed in the back corner. Still, she could think of much more entertaining ways for the two of them to use up their time in Vegas than just waiting around. His body, fresh and clean and smelling of soap; those arms wrapped strongly around her like they'd been when he'd tried to keep her from decapitating Evan... No. This was serious.

He snagged a t-shirt from the closet and pulled it over his head as he moved toward the seating area and gestured her toward an armchair. "What's on your mind? Need anything to drink?"

"No, thanks." She sank into the chair, glad that she didn't have to stand for this. She hadn't told anyone beyond her immediate family and clan members. She hadn't even wanted *them* to know; it was just too embarrassing. But anyone who was going to spend a lot of time with her needed to know the truth. Folks didn't expect people in wheelchairs to walk down a set of stairs, and other shifters shouldn't expect her to suddenly turn into an animal.

"Not even coffee?" He picked up the carafe from the machine in the kitchenette and poured himself a mugful.

"It's kind of late for that, isn't it?" She smiled, glad for the distraction, but knowing it was only prolonging the inevitable.

"Not when you drink as much of it as I do. I haven't had nearly enough in the past twenty-four hours, so I figured this was a good time to do a little catching up." He sat down, their chairs separated by a small, round table. His brow wrinkled in concern. "I'm sure you want to know what's next. I've called in all the details I can, including the vehicle description and everything Evan told us. We'll find him."

"But—"

"No, we will." He held up his hand to keep her from arguing, even though she hadn't intended to argue with him at all. "Annie, I've been on extraction missions in foreign countries where we have far fewer resources. Whatever Evan intended, and whoever these other guys are who have him, they're not going to get away with it. They don't seem to realize that not only are they dealing with a Hollywood star whose face would be recognized almost anywhere, but a guy who has the SOS Force at his back."

"I know, and I believe you." Annie sensed that he needed to hear that, although she didn't understand why. Jude was strong and capable, and the reassurance of someone like her shouldn't matter. She cleared her throat. "There's actually something else I wanted to talk to you about."

"All right." Jude waved his hand for her to go on as he took a sip from his mug.

Could she do this? He might not be romantically interested in her, but overall, Jude was a good guy. He'd asked her to trust him. "You noticed earlier that I didn't shift when we were fighting off Evan's men," she began. "I know that wasn't exactly the normal thing for people like us."

"It's okay," he said softly, leaning forward and torturing her with his proximity and his kindness. "I know this has been a very stressful situation."

"Let me finish, please. I know that wasn't exactly normal, but neither am I. I...I can't shift." The words hung in the air between them. Annie couldn't take them back, but she wondered how well he'd respond to them.

"You can't?"

"Nope."

He took another long, slow sip of coffee. "Have you ever been able to shift, or is it just right now?"

Annie knew what he meant. Sometimes, if a shifter was very ill or very stressed, it made that basic function extremely difficult. "I've never been in any form other than the one you see right now."

His eyes flicked down her body and back to her face. "Why?"

She lifted a shoulder. "I really don't know. Mom and Dad were always kind about it, but I could tell they were upset. I'm not like all the other shifters, and I'm sure it was a big disappointment for them, especially because of our Alpha bloodline. There aren't a lot of doctors who can help with this sort of thing, but the few specialists they took me to didn't really have any answers. They said it just happens sometimes." Now that she'd popped the cork, it was all coming out in a flood. "I'm really sorry. I should've told you earlier. I was coming out here with the intention of helping you with this mission, but I'm not the kind of help you were expecting."

Jude's face twitched as emotions flashed over it. "There's nothing to apologize for, Annie. I'm glad you were able to tell me. I'm sure this hasn't been easy for you."

She let out a short laugh that brought a few tears with it, and she blinked them away as quickly as possible. "To say the least. This was exactly why I was so worried about Jordan being gone all the time and leaving me in charge. It's an honor, but it doesn't do me much good when they don't think of me as one of them."

"The clan members give you trouble over this?" His fingers were entwined in front of him, his knuckles white. Perhaps this revelation was bothering him more than he was letting on.

"Some of them, yes. It's made me worry a lot about the future leadership of the clan. I don't want anyone to question Jordan just because his sister is a weirdo. He promised me we'd figure some things out when he got back, and now I don't know if he'll ever *be* back. I don't know what's going to happen to me or all the people I care about." The patterned carpet blurred in front of her eyes as the tears came in a flood.

"It's all right." Jude was at her side, his arm wrapped warmly around her, his fingers tracing over her bare skin just below her shirt sleeve. "That's a lot to think about. I'm really sorry you're having to go through all that."

His words only brought her more pain. Annie knew he was just saying those things because he felt like he had to. As much as she wanted to lean into his embrace and tell him her other secret, she knew it could never happen. It was right of her to tell him the truth about never shifting, but explaining her feelings would only complicate things.

Jude got up and came back a moment later with a box of tissues. "Would it be all right if I asked you a few more questions?"

"Sure." What did she have to lose, after all? Jude knew what only a handful of other people did.

"I don't know how it feels for you, but I can feel my bear inside. When I'm in my human form, it's like there's an animal living just under the surface of my skin. Is it the same for you?"

"Yes." It sure as hell was, and that damn bear had been going berserk every time Jude was around. It still wouldn't calm down, even though she'd already told herself she wasn't going to do anything about her feelings for Jude.

"Do you know if there are others like you?"

Annie flooded one tissue and snagged a second one. "It was implied, back when I was a kid and my parents took me to those specialists. They said it was rare, though."

"I see. And I suppose that means you don't know if anyone ever manages to get past this."

"I mean, I'm twenty-five years old and I've never been able to do it. What could possibly change now?" Her face was swelling from all the crying. She could feel it, and she knew that meant it was also turning some interesting shades of purple and red. Great.

"It was just a thought. I don't know what the procedure is like for something like this." He had his hand on her back now, running it smoothly up and down her spine. "We've got a few excellent doctors on the Force who might be able to help: one in D.C., and one in L.A. I understand there's another shifter doctor affiliated with our Dallas unit, too. Maybe she knows something about it."

Annie shook her head. "Maybe. I don't know. I'm not sure I could handle getting hopeful and going through a bunch of tests just to get let down again." She easily remembered all those late-night conversations she'd heard when she'd snuck out of her bedroom as a kid, with her mother crying and her father murmuring reassurances. Eventually, Jordan had been brought in on those meetings, too. They were talking about her, how she was different, and what it would mean for their family for the future. She hated it.

"What if the two of us worked on it? Together?"

Swiping a tissue across her eyes, she finally looked up at him. "What?"

"It's going to be difficult for us to know what to do next about Jordan until I get more information from headquarters. We could spend all night visiting the casinos, hoping we happen to bump into him, but the chance of that happening is slim to none. Instead, we could see if there's anything we can do to find that bear inside you."

It was a sweet offer, but she didn't think it was going to do any good. "Jude, that's kind of you. But I've tried about a million times. Jordan used to take me out into the woods, telling me he'd find a way to make it work for me. He'd get all excited with this plan for me to perfect my shifting without telling anyone and then have me suddenly drop into full bear mode at the dinner table as a way of telling our parents. Obviously, that never worked. My parents tried, too, as well as a few other senior clan members they trusted. It just isn't going to happen."

He nodded and sat back in his chair, sipping his coffee. "I understand. I'm sure you've tried a lot of different things, but I want to help in any way I can. You're obviously unhappy, and I want to make it better."

Annie couldn't understand why he'd care so much, but he was the only option she had at the moment. He'd gone out of his way for her, and if he truly wanted to do this, then she could give a little. "All right. What do you want to do?"

Jude set his mug aside and stood up with far more ease and energy than a man who'd had a day like theirs should've had. "Get a good pair of shoes on. We'll go out to Red Rock Canyon."

"What?" Despite how hard she'd been crying, she wanted to laugh now. "Can't we just close the curtains and try it here?"

He gave her a look that was gentle but also said he meant business. Jude was good at that. "I'm personally not interested in drawing any more atten-tion to ourselves than we might already have with our activities at Evan's place. This could get loud and possibly destructive, and that would be hard to explain."

Annie's cheeks colored, thinking of just what their hotel neighbors might think if they were in there roaring and thrashing about. "I guess that's true."

"Personally, I've also found it to be helpful to be out in the middle of nowhere. We live in a world full of humanity, but that makes it hard to tap into that wild side of ourselves. It's at least worth a try."

Jordan had already tried getting her into the outdoors for this, but that had been a long time ago. "All right. I'll be back in a second."

She went back through the doorway to her room and found a pair of sneakers. She was exhausted from all the emotions she'd already gone through that day, and she could feel it in her bones. Despite her best intentions to keep herself at bay, she was happy to have an excuse to spend more time with Jude, and they were soon on their way back out to the edge of the city.

He parked the car in the deepest shadows just off the road and headed into the park with eagerness in his step. "Tell me what methods you've tried before."

She skirted the scrubby bushes and followed him into the rocky outcropping that took up the area. "Oh, lots of things. Meditating. Spending time with others in their bear forms. Wearing talismans that were supposed to have the spirit of the bear inside them. Getting drunk."

"Really?"

"That last one was Jordan's idea," she said with a smile. "He thought I just didn't know how to relax. He wasn't totally wrong about that, but the only thing I got out of it was a hangover."

"Other than drinking, those were probably all good methods. I can't say that I know the perfect solution, but I imagine this is sort of like teaching someone to walk after they've been in a bad accident. We don't know how to teach something so intrinsic."

"That makes me feel a lot better." She was grateful for the darkness so Jude couldn't see her scowl. This was a stupid idea. She was already embarrassed, and she hadn't even tried yet.

"I just mean that it makes it difficult. Would you be able to tell someone how to blink?"

"No, I don't suppose I would." Annie blinked, acutely aware of the motion now that he'd brought it up, but still unable to describe it.

"Humans have physical therapists who've gone through a lot of training to know how to help someone learn to walk a second time. We don't have anything like that in the shifter world that I know of;

I'll have to talk to our resident doc, Emersyn, about it sometime. Anyway, I guess I'll just start by trying to explain everything I do when I shift."

"Okay." It seemed incredibly intimate for him to tell her such a thing, especially since it wasn't something she shared.

They moved further into the park before he finally came to a stop in a small valley created by the rocks. It shut off the lights from the city, making the stars overhead sparkle brilliantly in the deep black sky. "I guess the first thing I do is reach down inside and get in touch with my bear. It's always there, and sometimes it's closer to the surface than usual. Sometimes I can hardly keep it at bay. But it's like I'm telling this other thing that lives inside of me that it's allowed to come out. Over the years, I've been able to do this with just a deep breath."

Annie pulled air into her lungs and closed her eyes, envisioning the beast she knew was inside her. It responded, confused, but it didn't exactly come bursting forth. "Okay. What else?"

"The bear and I are the same being, yet we're not. It's like I'm not only giving it permission to come out, but assuring it I won't be hurt if it does. My human part just goes to the inside, like they trade places."

"That makes sense." Annie imagined what that

must feel like, a human curled up inside a great bear. She'd fantasized about it plenty of times, but that had never made it happen before. "What's next?"

"Well..." He trailed off. "Shit. This is harder than I thought. I'm sorry. I just never thought about it in this depth before."

"Don't worry about it, Jude. I appreciate it, but I don't want to waste any more of your time than I already have." Annie turned to go back the way they'd come.

"You don't get to give up that easily. I'll shift first, and I'll pay more attention. Then we can try it for you." He let go of her arm.

Annie watched as he filled his lungs with air. Jude made no other special movements that she could see, but as he exhaled, his human form began to fall away. Fur exploded over his body. His arms and legs grew thicker as he bent forth and stretched his fingers into paws and claws. Even in the darkness, he was a magnificent beast. She hesitantly stepped forward.

Jude watched her, his green eyes now dark but welcoming, like a deep emerald velvet. Anyone who didn't know the truth about him would think he was just a wild beast, but in those eyes, she could see he was something completely different. Though she'd grown up surrounded by bears, he wasn't like the others. She reached out and touched the top of his head, gently at first, hesitantly, wondering if this was really okay. Jude tipped his muzzle up, encouraging her. She stroked his ears and down his neck, in awe of that strange pattern in the fur covering his chest. As much as she appreciated his beauty from a human standpoint, she longed to see what he was like as a fellow bear.

He seemed to know this, and he nudged his big black nose against her side. Annie nodded, hoping beyond all hope that she could do this. So many times in her life, she'd been left behind because she couldn't be what her genes told her she should be. This was one thing she didn't want to miss out on.

Stepping back to give herself a little space, Annie got in touch with her inner bear. *It's all right to come out. You've been hiding for so long, and I know you want to be free. You won't hurt me. We'll just change places for a little while.* Annie sucked in a deep breath and let it out.

Nothing happened. Though she mentally commanded her body to change, it refused to do so. There were no twisting bones or relocating organs, and she had no more hair than she'd woken up with that morning. She was just a human. Annie sighed.

A cold nose on her thigh startled her, but it was just Jude. He watched her in earnest, commanding her with his silence to try again. Somehow, it was easier to try when he wasn't in his human form, like she wasn't being watched as closely. He'd already shifted in front of her, letting her see that strange in-between configuration that some shifters didn't like to share with others. That was one way in which he'd opened up to her. Annie found herself constantly owing him, but never in a way that felt like a burden.

She nodded. Jude had told her about taking one deep breath, but maybe she just wasn't strong enough to do it that way. Annie sucked in air, visualizing it as the bear side of herself coming in. Every outward breath was her human side leaving, and the more she breathed, the more ursine she should become.

Ideally. After standing there for what felt like an hour, she was still human. "I'm sorry."

Jude turned away from her as he shed his bear form. It looked so easy for him to command his body as his shaggy brown coat receded into his skin and his face folded and flattened into the one she was familiar with. "Don't be sorry. It's not like I expected it to happen right away, and you shouldn't either."

Annie balled her fists at her sides. She'd already cried enough for the day, yet she felt tears prickling her eyes once again. "Maybe this wasn't the best time for me to bring this up. I've got too much on my mind."

"That's completely understandable. Don't give up on yourself just yet, though. Shifting is a big thing. Maybe we need to look at it like eating an elephant."

"Huh?" She looked up at him, silhouetted against the stars. Jude was so perfect. He'd served the country and now served his fellow shifters, and he carried it all out while looking like he belonged on the cover of *GQ*.

He smiled. "It's a big project, and you have to do it one bite at a time. Come over here and sit." Jude brought her to a large boulder.

She sat next to him, surprised when he took her arm in his hand and turned it over to reveal her inner wrist. His fingers were warm and gentle, but she could sense that inner strength in him.

"We think of shifting as the entire body all at once, but it isn't always like that. I've had times when I didn't want to shift, but I was getting so riled up about something that part of me started to change.

Say, for instance, suddenly having a lot more hair on the back of my neck."

Annie laughed. "That could be inconvenient in a business meeting."

"You're telling me! Try this. Focus just on this part of your body, this thinner skin right here. Imagine what it would feel like to have your fur come straight through the skin. That's what it feels like. It isn't as though it regrows every time; it just forces its way through."

She kept her eyes on her arm, not daring to look up at his face when they were so close to each other. She wanted him so badly. He was sexy, yes, but it was so much more than that. He wanted to help her find Jordan, and he wanted to fix a problem she'd had her entire life. It was a far bigger task than one man could possibly handle, yet he wasn't ready to give up on her. He was the perfect man, and that only made her all the sadder for not being able to have him.

"What about the skin?" she asked quietly. "Does it just stay in the same spot?"

"It seems to. It grows and changes when your whole body shifts, but that's nothing you'll notice if you work on just this part. Concentrate on each hair and what it must feel like. Don't worry about anything else."

It was easier said than done, but she tried. She envisioned a humiliating amount of hair suddenly erupting from her skin, each hair tickling as it poked its way through.

But once again, nothing happened.

7

"Let's take a break." The stars provided enough light for Jude to see the exhaustion in Annie's eyes. Her shoulders sagged, and she no longer wanted to stand up as she attempted the transformation, but that emotional drain was the worst part to witness.

"I really wanted to make this happen," she said pitifully, sitting down with a thump on a nearby rock. She bent forward and rested her forehead on her knees. "It seemed like a good backup plan, something that would help me run the clan if we can't find Jordan. I don't think it's ever going to happen."

"Come here." Using his foot to move a few rocks aside and even out the ground, Jude waved her over. "You're wiped out."

Annie pulled herself up and staggered over without protest. He thought she might just say they should go back to the hotel and get some rest, but Jude doubted either one of them would be able to sleep. "I'll rest, but I don't think it's going to help."

Jude laid down next to her. "You're just as stubborn as your brother, you know that?"

He heard her smirk more than he saw it. "So I've been told. What kind of stubbornness do you know in him?"

"Are there multiple kinds of stubborn? I wasn't aware that they could be categorized." He was smiling, too, so worn out from the past twenty-four hours that he wasn't sure if even he could shift at the moment.

"Oh, sure. There's the kind of stubborn he was when we were little kids, and he insisted he should be allowed to live in the woods by himself and hunt for his own meals."

"Seriously? Mr. Hollywood Hotshot wanted to do that?" Jude hadn't known Jordan until they were in their early teens, when childhood fantasies had been replaced by dreams of girls and fast cars.

"Yup. He even ran away once because he said the walls of the house were suffocating him. I guess Jordan was just super in touch with his bear then. I didn't understand at the time. I was happy to sleep in my bed instead of out on the ground."

"And now?" Jude was incredibly comfortable despite the hardness of the earth beneath them.

Apparently, Annie felt the same way. "With everything going on in my life, it's kind of nice to just *be*. I don't get a lot of chances to do that."

"I'm sure it's difficult being in charge of everyone like you are." He couldn't truly understand her clan life. Jude had been adopted into a clan, but wasn't the same. Jude, Reid, and the Hoffmans didn't live in the clubhouse or have much to do with the day-to-day operations of the members.

"When they let me be. Jude, I really appreciate you bringing me out here and helping me with this. You didn't have to."

Yes, he did, but he wasn't going to say it out loud. He had to do it not because he had some sort of obligation to her that she might be offended by, but because he knew there was a deep connection between them. He had to do it because he wanted to do it, because he wanted her to have every possible chance at happiness. He wanted everything for her that she didn't have, and all that she deserved. "It's no problem."

"Can I ask you something, though? About your bear?"

"Sure." He liked just laying there with her, staring up at the stars, pretending they were the only two people in the universe. Jude would talk all night long if it meant they didn't have to go back to reality.

"When you shifted, I saw a mark on your chest. This silvery little swirl. What is that? I'm sorry if it's something I shouldn't be asking. I've just never seen anything like it before."

If it was anyone else, Jude might've been embarrassed. But it was Annie, and it was different. "I don't know. Some sort of birthmark, I guess, because I've always had it."

She rolled up onto her elbow so that she was looking down at him, outlined by the stars. "Is it...Is it there when you're in this form?" Her finger swayed, vaguely pointing at his chest.

Jude's gut contracted against his spine, excited that she might even remotely be thinking about his body. "No, it's not." he replied quietly. "Annie?"

"Yes?"

This was a mistake. He knew it even before he said it, but she'd opened up to him and told him something that no shifter would willingly admit to another. She'd made herself vulnerable, and it was time for him to do the same. "I know it was tough for you to tell me about not being able to shift. You were carrying that around and felt like I had the right to know."

She looked away toward their feet, embarrassed again. "I'm sorry if it bothers you."

"No, Annie." He sat up, pulling her with him and taking her hands in his. "What I'm saying is that there's something I've been carrying around, too. I don't know if I should tell you or not, because I don't know what consequences it'll bring, but I will if you'll let me."

She looked up at him, excitement and intrigue in her eyes. "Of course you can."

Jude swallowed. Jordan would kill him once they found him. He might be grateful to Jude for taking care of his sister, but this was crossing the line. Still, they were in the middle of nowhere, and there could be no repercussions from anyone but her right now. "Annie, I'm crazy about you. Every time I'm around you, I can feel something change inside me. It's like my bear goes absolutely wild with the urge to be with you, but it isn't just physical. I'm in love with every part of you, your body and your soul."

She squinted at him with disbelief. "You are?"

"Yes, and I know it's not right for me to say this. I

know you're from an Alpha bloodline and Jordan is my best friend, but I can't deny the way I feel about you anymore. What you do to me is what all the other shifters talk about. You give me that innate, deep-rooted sensation that I've finally met the person I'm supposed to be with. Annie, I don't want this to scare you or make you feel like you have some sort of obligation toward me. I just want you to know that I love you."

Annie was as still as a statue, her face illuminated by the stars as she stared at him, her lips slightly parted in a look of wonder. "I feel the same way about you. I love you, too, Jude." Her voice was thick with tears, but they weren't the same tears she'd cried over Jordan or over her frustration with her body. "I always just thought of you as my brother's friend, and I thought you were cute, but for the longest time, it didn't go any deeper than that. Then it was like everything changed in the matter of a second, one of those times that you were on leave from the Army and hanging out at our house. I didn't think that could be possible, that I'd suddenly feel something I hadn't felt before. Not being able to shift made me doubt myself even more. If I couldn't become who I was supposed to be, then how could I actually be feeling that? Was it even fair of me to feel that way toward you when I couldn't shift?"

"I don't care about any of that. I've known shifters who've found their mates in people who aren't shifters at all."

"So..." She trailed off, her breath coming heavily and heaving her chest as she watched him, waiting.

Jude lifted a hand and skimmed it along her jawline, pressing his lips to hers. He closed his eyes and let himself fall into it, pushing away all the worry. He'd had concerns about what his feelings for her would mean in the real world, and so did she, but the real world could wait.

Her lips were soft and warm, inviting him in. She opened her mouth and deepened the kiss in a way far more intimate than he'd imagined it could be. Annie explored his mouth, showing him her hunger and desire for him.

His bear was in utter bliss as Jude grabbed her by the waist and pulled her onto his lap. Annie's legs wrapped around him easily, a small whimper of desperation for him escaping her lips as she ran her hands down his back and skimmed them under the hem of his shirt, igniting all his pulse points in glorious energy.

For a moment, he let his guilt wash over him.

"Annie," he breathed as he moved his mouth along her jaw and down the delicate curve of her neck. "You don't have to." But God, did he want her to. He crushed his arm around her waist, holding her tightly against him and never wanting to let go.

"I *want* to," she whispered back, pulling his shirt over his head. "I've wanted you for so long, Jude."

His desire was a burning fire that blazed through the marrow of his bones, buzzing in his blood. He slowly stripped her clothing away, wanting to touch every inch of her. From the bend of her elbow and the hard roundness of her knee to the curve of her hips and the swell of her breasts, every part of her was enticing. The anticipation of what would come next left him tingling down to the tips of his toes.

"I want *you*," he said as he dragged his tongue along her shoulder and moved the strap of her bra aside, knowing what he needed. He laid her down on the sandy ground, stripping her bra and panties off so that she lay naked before him. Not vulnerable, but glorious. Jude grazed the tan line that ran from her shoulder to the top of her breast and then further, teasing her nipple with his tongue as she tangled one hand in his hair.

Her other hand was free, and it roved over his shoulder and down his arm, her fingertips exploring the curves and valleys of his muscles. She moved further down, spreading her fingers across his abdomen and down between his legs, touching, lingering. Jude's body had already been ready to go, but she elicited a low moan from him as she curled her fingers around his eager shaft.

"Fuck," he grunted, trying so hard to control himself. That'd been the game ever since he'd jumped in his car and gone to meet her at her house. She made him not want to control himself at all, to act like the wild beast he'd been suppressing for so long.

She caressed his shoulder with her lips, moving up his neck and to his ear, where she swept the tip of her tongue against his lobe. Her right hand continued its play between his legs, stroking, exploring, asking.

"Annie." Jude lowered himself into her, scooping his arms around her back and holding her against him, savoring the moment. They were joined physically, but he knew this was far more than that. She was warm and soft around him and underneath him, and Jude didn't want it ever to end.

As much as this was feeding their souls, their bodies had demands that had to be met. Her hips thrust against him as they moved in perfect rhythm. She was heaven and earth, right there in his arms.

Annie pressed her hips upward and arched her back, compressing herself against him. He could feel her body shivering from the inside out, which only drove him to work harder. He thrust faster, hoping to stave himself off as long as possible.

Her legs wrapped around him, pulling him tighter against her, and a moan of pleasure escaped her lips. Gripping his shoulders with her hands as she moved against him, she threw her head back and cried out into the night. Her ecstasy echoed against the rocks that surrounded them and up into the stars as her body constricted in ripples of pleasure.

Jude followed quickly in her footsteps, thrilled to see such contentment playing across her features. He held her tightly as he came, his entire body focusing on their connection before he let go. He worried he might crush her in his grip as everything he'd felt for her, everything he'd been pressing down inside himself, came shooting to the surface.

She lay next to him, peeking up shyly over his shoulder. "I had no idea. About how you felt, I mean."

"Am I that mysterious?"

"Yeah," she replied instantly. "If you've actually been feeling the way you say you have, then you're an expert at hiding it."

He leaned over and kissed her. "It sure as hell hasn't been easy."

Annie moved her head up onto his chest. "I think we both needed this. I know we have a lot to go back to and a lot of work ahead of us, but I'm glad we were able to get away from it all for a bit."

Jude laughed. "Do you know how crazy people would think we are? We're right here next to one of the top destinations in the country and have top-notch hotel rooms, but we're laying out here on the ground in the middle of nowhere. It's better like this, or at least I think it is." He was enjoying the shared warmth of their bodies, the feeling of being naked under the sky, the euphoria of being with Annie, and finally getting the chance to tell her the truth.

"I think so, too." She settled in more closely at his side. "Do you ever look up at the stars and wonder how many other shifters are doing the same thing at the same time? I know it sounds stupid, like something out of a movie, but I've always thought there was a certain kind of magic to them."

"Absolutely." He put his arm around her, wanting to just hold onto her forever. Annie was like a drug he couldn't get enough of, and it was an addiction he was enjoying. "My mom died when I was really young, but she always used to talk to me about the stars. She said that Ursa Major was the first great bear and that it represented all the bear shifters in the world. It was like a celestial representation of us, someone we could always look up to even when we didn't have another bear around."

"That sounds a lot more romantic than just calling it the Big Dipper." Annie looked up with him, her hair falling over his chest and tickling his throat.

He liked it, though. "Ursa Minor is up there for all the bears who don't quite know who they are or what their destiny is yet. It was always one of my favorite constellations to find as a kid. I felt like I was seeing myself up there in the stars." Jude looked back to Ursa Major, thinking about his mother. She'd said the stars that made up the pattern represented all the bear shifters who'd ever lived. He knew now, as an adult, that it'd all been metaphorical, but he couldn't help but wonder if she'd been watching over him all these years.

"No one ever told me that," Annie said, sounding wistful. "Everything was about meetings and business and checking the books. My parents had a very corporate view of the clan. I thought Jordan would handle things a little differently. He does, but it's still not the way I'd run the ship."

"And what would you do?" He leaned his head to the side, pressing his cheek against her scalp.

"It doesn't really matter," she hedged.

"Sure it does."

Annie moved her head to look up at him. "You give me too much credit, Jude."

"Then maybe you should take it."

"All right. If I were to run the clan, I'd want it to be a bit of the casual side that Jordan likes and a bit of the more organized side that my parents preferred. I've spent too much time trying to make up for Jordan's lack of management, and maybe that's part of what made everyone resent me so much." She frowned, laying her head back down on his chest.

He stroked her hair. It felt so intimate, even considering what they'd just done. Jude noted that his bear was quiet and content. Every time he'd been near her, it'd gone crazy. They were as close as possible now, but it'd finally gotten what it needed. "I doubt they resent you."

Annie was quiet as she looked up at the stars. "I resented myself. I was angry at myself for not being what everyone else expected me to be, but I can see now that those expectations were probably all from me, too. I've spent so much time being acutely aware of how different I am and paying such close attention to it, that I don't give anyone else a chance to be close to me."

"I know how difficult family relations are." He was proud of her for making such a breakthrough, but he knew the same thing wouldn't come for him. Jude was an orphan. There was no one to make up with. He and Reid had a good relationship, and Annie was the only other person who mattered.

Her body had been still, but Annie suddenly shoved up off his chest and was scrambling to her feet.

"What's wrong?" He listened, tapping into his animal's senses. All was quiet around them.

"Nothing. I want to try again." She stood before him, naked and glorious, grinning from ear to ear.

"Annie, you don't have to do that."

But she was giggling now. "Yes, I do. Jude, you make me feel more alive than I've ever felt before. So many times, I've tried to get closer with my bear, trying to get it to come out and play for a while. I couldn't do it, but there's something about being out here with you in the way that we are that just feels different."

Before he could offer any advice, Annie had sucked in a deep breath that thrust her breasts forward. She tipped her head back into the starlight, and her shoulders sagged. Jude got to his feet, worried something had gone wrong. She fell forward, bracing herself on all fours as her back lengthened, muscles and fur blooming all over her body. Her beautiful face molded and changed into that of a bear. He watched in fascination as her ears rounded over and moved up to the top of her head.

"You're beautiful," he said as he approached her, admiring the flecks of gold and black in her fur. "This is the part of you I was able to see even when you couldn't show it to the rest of the world."

She looked up at him with her ursine eyes, which were the same rich color as her human ones. Annie nudged his hip with her cold nose.

He smiled, knowing what she wanted. "Yeah. Let's do this." Jude stepped back and shifted, molding and forming into his own version of what Annie had now become. As good as it'd felt to be human with her, being in their true forms together was remarkable. There was a certain connection that simply wasn't there when they stood on two feet.

Jude noticed an odd vibration coming from her. *Are you all right?*

Yeah. It's a little scary, and I'm not used to it yet, but I finally know who I am. Annie turned her nose toward her left flank and then her right, trying to see the entirety of herself. *I'm glad you're here with me.*

Me, too. The two of them ambled off into the night, leaving their clothes in a pile behind them, picking up speed as they ran through the canyons and used them as their playground.

8

———

L.A. SEEMED TOO FAMILIAR AS ANNIE AND JUDE pulled away from the airport. While their trip to Vegas wasn't intended to be a vacation at all, she'd liked being somewhere different with him. It was nice to get away from everything she'd known before. If she hadn't, she might never have found the other side of herself.

Of course, coming back to L.A. also meant having to face the awful fact that Jordan was still missing. "When do you think you'll hear back about that vehicle?"

Jude kept his eyes on the road. "It just depends. There's no certain timeline, but I'm sure they'll find it. I'll go to headquarters and help with the search."

"If we need to go back to Vegas, I'd be happy to

join you," she said with a smile. Their night under the stars had been absolutely sublime. Annie couldn't have asked for anything more spontaneous and romantic, and she'd been reliving it the entire plane ride back. Her body was still tingling with all the energy, both from her time with Jude and from finally being able to shift. She'd tapped into a part of herself that'd always been there but refused to come to the surface, and she knew she'd never be the same again.

"We'll just have to see what happens," he replied noncommittally. "It might be too dangerous."

Annie sank into the passenger seat. Jude had gone back to that quiet, stoic façade he'd put up before they'd gone out to Red Rock Canyon. Somehow, she imagined it would be different between the two of them now, but she'd been wrong. "Is everything okay? I mean, between us?"

His jaw tightened, and her stomach sank. Something was definitely not okay.

"Please, Jude. Just talk to me."

He flicked on the turn signal but still wouldn't look at her. "I've been thinking a lot about what happened between us. I was being honest when I told you what I'd been feeling for you, and I'm glad that we both got that off our chests. But I still don't feel right about betraying Jordan."

"He's not going to care." Annie believed that, but she could see the little fantasy world she'd so quickly built up around herself and Jude crumbling to pieces. They'd had a magical night, running through the canyons and bluffs, being themselves and being together. They hadn't come back to retrieve their clothes until dawn, and when they'd gone to the hotel, they'd tumbled into his bed.

"You say that. Annie, I know you're a pretty realistic person, but things are different between guys. I saw the way Jordan was always trying to keep you away from the wrong guys, and how much he worried about you." His knuckles turned white on the steering wheel.

"That doesn't mean you!" Annie felt anger rising in her system at the notion, bringing back those same old feelings of frustration and defeat. She couldn't possibly have come this far, only to have the one person who truly understood her turn around and let it all go.

"It does. Trust me, Annie. I know it does. When we find Jordan, if he finds out what happened between us, he'll never speak to me again. I can handle that, but I don't want to ruin any relationship the two of you have. Family is more important than anything."

"No, it's not!" Her voice filled the car. She could hear that shrill quality that always came through when she got frustrated with her clan when they refused to do what was best for them. Everything she'd longed and hoped for was being yanked out from under her. "You can't possibly sit there and tell me that a fated connection, something so deep and special that you can only share it with it one other person in the entire world, is more important than anything else!"

He glanced at her and then back at the road, bracing one elbow on the door and propping his head on his hand. "You don't understand."

"Then make me," she growled. "Don't sit there and talk to me like you know so much more than I do just because you've been able to shift your entire life, and I've only been able to do it for a day."

"It's not about that. Damn it." Jude sighed. "I don't want Jordan to think I took advantage of you when you were vulnerable, nor do I want you to look back on the situation and think the same thing. That's not all of it, though."

"You might as well tell me, then, because all my patience went out the window about half a mile back." Annie put her tongue between her teeth and bit down just hard enough to keep herself from crying again. This emotional roller coaster was more than she could handle.

"Annie, you come from a prominent bloodline of Alphas. Your clan has been handed down from one generation to the next for as far back as anyone can remember. If shifters had royalty, you'd be part of it."

She'd never thought about it like that, but she still didn't see how it was relevant. "Your point?"

"I have absolutely no business being with you. I was lucky enough to get adopted into a clan when my parents passed away, but I was always on the outskirts. I've been the black sheep my entire life. If you're going to be with someone, it needs to be somebody who deserves that position."

Annie's mouth fell open as she tried to wrap her head around what he was saying. "Are you seriously telling me you don't deserve me?"

"Don't bother telling me it's not true. You might not see it right now, but in time you will, and you'll be glad that I backed out of this before it was too late." He turned into the driveway in front of the Martinez clan's clubhouse.

"I can't fucking believe you, Jude," Annie said bitterly, feeling betrayed. "I opened up to you. I told you everything that I'd been going through, and you seemed to understand. I guess you just used that to get what you wanted out of me." She unfastened her seatbelt and let the buckle fly back, knocking into the post. When she got out of the car, she slammed the door behind her. All the violence in the world wasn't going to make her feel any better about this.

Jude got out of the car as well, moving carefully and wearing that same neutral look on his face. He reached for the trunk, but she slapped his hand away.

"I can get it myself, thank you very much." Somehow, her suitcase had grown far heavier in the two days since she'd left L.A. Her anger fueled her strength, however, and she whipped it out and onto the sidewalk.

"Annie, I understand if you're mad. I just want you to recognize where I'm coming from." He stood there by the trunk like he was waiting for her to change her mind and say it was all fine.

"Oh, don't worry. I understand *completely*." Annie stepped up close to him, not because she wanted to be near him, but because she didn't want to risk anyone overhearing what she had to say. "You've had a little time to think about it, and you don't want to put up with the embarrassment of being with me. I might be able to shift now, but I'm still not as worthy as someone who's been able to do it all along. I don't fit in with your Special Ops Shifter Force bros and all the superhero shit you do. And you know what? That's absolutely fine with me, Jude." She turned on her heel and marched up the walkway.

"Annie! It's not like that!"

She ignored him, and by the time she was letting herself in the side door, she heard him getting back into his car. Part of her was upset that he didn't follow her and try to argue his case anymore. She wanted to argue with him. She wanted to yell and scream and punch him in his stupid, perfectly-chiseled face. But there wouldn't be a chance to do that. After all, he wasn't arguing in favor of them being together. Jude didn't want to have anything to do with her.

The only thing she wanted to do was get up to her room and collapse into bed, but as she turned for the hall, she nearly ran into Austin.

"Hey! There you are! How was Oregon?"

"What?" she snapped, not wanting to deal with him.

"You said you went to Oregon to visit your sick friend or something," he reminded her.

The hallway was too close. Annie thought she

might suffocate if they stood there much longer, and she didn't really give a shit what Austin or anyone else thought of her. The universe had let her down. "Yeah, well, I lied. I went to Vegas to look for Jordan." She pushed past him.

Austin followed her into the living room. "Whoa, hold on. Did you find him?"

Annie stopped and sighed, her breath hot in her mouth. This was one of the many aspects of returning to real life that she hadn't been anticipating. Until they found Jordan, she was still in charge. She'd spoken to Jude about dumb ideas like balancing the way she ran the place, but with the way she felt right now, she just didn't give a shit. "Why would you care? I came to you when he didn't come back from his shoot, and you told me he was probably just hanging out with some showgirls. I was the only person in this damn house who wanted to make sure he was all right."

"I'm sorry about that." Austin took her suitcase from her hand and put it in the corner. "Sit down. You look really upset."

The last thing she wanted was for a man like him to patronize her. Even as upset as she was with Jude, she wasn't going to just fall into his arms. That was probably what he was hoping for; he was always trying to find a way to get under her skin. The fact remained, however, that Austin was one of the most senior members of their clan. Just like the Martinezes, his family had been around for generations. If anyone deserved to know, it was him. Still. "Is Michelle around?"

He shook his head. "She went to the store and out to run some errands. She knew you were coming back today, and she didn't want you to be upset if things hadn't been handled around here." He smiled at her.

Annie turned away from him, not wanting to see anyone give her that look. His smile wasn't anything genuine anyway. It was just another way he was kissing her ass. She sank down onto the sofa. "An old friend of mine said he'd help me find Jordan. We went to Las Vegas, since that was the last place he'd been seen. We didn't find him, but someone thought they saw him. It turned out to be his stunt double."

"Oh. So, is he really missing, then?" Austin sat down too close to her, but she had no room to scoot away.

"That seems to be the case. The worst part is that this stunt double was a human, and his plan was to take over Jordan's career. He found out about Jordan being a shifter, and he ended up selling him to some other guys. I'm just waiting for a little more information so I can figure out what to do next." Annie stood, feeling claustrophobic, and went to the window. She craved the wide-open space she and Jude had found out in Red Rock Canyon, though she didn't want to share it with him or anyone else.

Austin followed her. "Information? Is this that guy that was with you out in the gazebo? I don't know anything about him, Annie, but you shouldn't trust him with clan information. That could be dangerous."

She gripped the windowsill, thinking about how wonderful it'd felt to let her claws free. "He's not dangerous." Not physically. And Jude wouldn't do anything to betray Jordan. That could be counted as a point in his favor if he hadn't used it as an excuse to stomp all over her heart.

"What kind of information are you waiting on? Maybe it's something I can help with."

Annie shook her head. Austin could probably hold his own in a bar room brawl, but he didn't have the same resources that Jude did. It wasn't like they could just drop in a few of the local hotspots and hope to find Jordan sitting at the bar somewhere. "The stunt double gave us a description of the vehicle, and it's being tracked down."

"What kind of vehicle?"

She felt her shoulders tense with irritation. Annie didn't need an inquisition like this right now. It would've been better to wait until she could gather everyone together and tell them all at once. "It's just a black Jeep, okay?"

Her eyes lifted as she said it, resting on a black Jeep parked in the driveway. She'd been so furious with Evan that she'd hardly even heard the description of her brother's captors, but now she could remember it as though the stuntman was whispering it in her ear at that moment. *A big blonde guy with a black Jeep.* Surely not...

She turned, finding that Austin had closed in on her. He put his hands on either side of the window frame, pinning her against the glass. "You really shouldn't stick your nose where it doesn't belong, Annie."

Panic flooded her system. "What the hell are you doing, Austin?"

"What I should've done a long time ago." In one swift movement, he snatched her wrists and twisted her arms around behind her back. Austin pulled her close so that he spoke right in her ear. "I thought I could do it the nice way, Annie. I was going to convince you that the two of us were meant to be together. After all, no one else would want a reject like you. It was supposed to be easy. You had to be stubborn, though."

Annie swallowed. "I don't understand. You're mad at me because I wouldn't go out with you?"

He shook her arms, making her head wobble painfully on her neck. "No, you stupid bitch! I never really wanted you, I was just sick and tired of seeing you and your incompetent brother lead this clan without a clue. Jordan didn't give a shit what happened because he was too caught up in his career, and you had so little of a life, you cared too much about what happened. I'd make a far better Alpha, and if I have to jump in and take the position, then so be it."

Rage and fear mixed nauseatingly in her stomach. "Austin, we can talk about this. Just let me go. If you want to have some hand in the administration of the clan, that can be done."

His laugh was sharp enough to crack through the room. "I was going to marry you and wait at least a year before I offed Jordan and took over for myself. I mean, we all know no one would tolerate you in the position, but my bond with you would solidify me as the Alpha. I'm not playing the long game anymore."

Fine. She'd tried to play nice and get him to talk.

It pissed Annie off to no end that she'd been right about Austin, yet no one had listened to her, but her complaints would have to wait. "Just tell me what you did with Jordan."

"Oh, you'll get to find out for yourself." Austin shoved her forward, back down the hall, and to the basement door. "You're lucky we didn't run into each other out in Vegas. I must have left right before you showed up at Evan's place. I figured your trip to Oregon would be the perfect time for me to head over to Nevada and pick up my prize." He opened the door.

Annie resisted, struggling against his grip. She let out a scream, one even louder than the one Jude had elicited from her back in the park, but just as primal.

Austin yanked hard, making her slam her head on the doorjamb. "Might as well keep your mouth shut, bitch. Anyone who's not on my side was sent out of the house for the night. No one who can hear you will be willing to help you." He dragged her down the stairs after him.

"What are you going to do with me?" she panted. Annie remembered Jude taking note of the fact that she hadn't shifted in the fight she'd helped him with. She dug down deep inside herself, hoping to find her bear and bring it out again. Her head spun from the blow, making it difficult to concentrate. No, it was best to wait. Let him think she was weak. He'd already made mention of 'what she was.'

"That remains to be seen. I think I'll play with you for a bit, and then I'll kill you. The only thing keeping me from doing it right now is coming up with a good cover story as to why both you and your brother disappeared. It shouldn't take much to convince the other members to elect me as their new Alpha. They already know I deserve it." Austin hauled her across the room, where one of his goons was waiting for her.

Annie looked up at Austin's accomplice. It was Mike, another man she'd known her entire life. He'd always hung out with Austin, but she'd never guessed he would be in on a scheme like this. "Mike, you don't have to do this. You don't have to do what he says."

But Mike smirked down at her. "I'm going to be his beta, so yeah, I do." He held her arms in place, crushing her biceps in his enormous hands as Austin fastened metal zip ties over her wrists.

"You'll be easy to dispatch when I get the chance later tonight since you're nothing but a weakling anyway, but there's nothing like a little precaution,"

Austin explained as he yanked them tight. "Even if you could shift, these would only cut off your circulation as soon as you became a bear."

He opened the door to a storage closet in the far corner of the basement and flicked on the light. Annie gasped as she saw a familiar figure already lying on the concrete floor. "Jordan!"

"You guys can have a little time to catch up before I get rid of you," Austin said. He shoved Annie into the room and slammed the door behind her.

Her knees hit the concrete, abrading through her thin jeans, and the metal strips bit into her wrists. Her heart was running solely on fear and adrenaline, and Annie scooted forward until she was next to her brother's crumpled form. "Jordan? Are you all right?"

"Oh, Annie. Oh, god. He got you, too. I'm so sorry. I'm so sorry for everything. I should've believed you."

With her hands bound uselessly behind her back, Annie bent forward and laid her head on his arm. "Yes, you should've, but I can berate you about that later. What is all this?"

Jordan struggled to sit up, using the wall behind him for leverage. He had a gash above his eye that was slowly seeping blood, and his facial hair had grown out into a thick stubble. "I'm still trying to figure it out. It started with my goddamn stunt double."

"I know about Evan," she offered. "When you didn't come home from Vegas, I started making phone calls. Austin wasn't concerned about your whereabouts, but now I know why. Anyway, I called Jude. He was going to help me find you."

"Jude?" Jordan whipped his head around to look at her. "Well, that was a pretty good choice."

"It turned out to be, even though I had no clue about this SOS Force stuff at the time. He and I went to Vegas to find you, and we found Evan instead. He told us about his plot to take over your career, but I'm afraid I didn't know until just now that it was Austin who'd come after you."

Jordan nodded. "Yeah. I called the clubhouse when I checked out, and I told Austin I was going out with Evan. My guess is that he figured it'd be easier to take me out in a strange place instead of the living room, but it didn't quite work out the way he planned."

"I wonder what's stopping him from killing us." Annie looked at the door. She'd heard Austin lock it behind him. Was he still on the other side of it, or had he gone upstairs? What had he done with the rest of the clan?

"It's a show for him," Jordan grunted, wriggling against his restraints. "He can't just slaughter us and take over. There are plenty of members who are content to just follow whomever the official Alpha is, but they're not going to stand for outright murder. Austin's trying to figure out his story."

"Which will be easy for him to do now that he's got us both down here. He told me he sent away everyone who wasn't in on his plan, too." Unwillingly, Annie wished Jude was there with them. That serene demeanor of his could be really useful right now.

"I'm sorry, Annie. You need to know that I'm really, really sorry. I'm sorry for being such a shitty Alpha. I'm sorry for not realizing how much you care about the clan. And I'm incredibly sorry for blowing you off when you said something was wrong. You know this clan better than anyone, and I should've listened to you." He turned to her, his handsome face twisted by grief.

"You're not a shitty Alpha," she said, feeling sorry both for him and herself. "We just have different ways of running the show, and it was difficult for us to make them both work."

"No. *I'm* difficult. And selfish. And look where it's gotten us." He bent his head to look over his shoulder at his bindings, which were the same as hers. "There's nothing I can do to get us out of this. I can't shift unless I want to lose circulation in my paws, and you can't possibly fight them on your own."

Annie bit her lip. She'd imagined giving Jordan the good news when they had a moment to themselves, maybe over dinner. There was no better time than now, especially since she didn't know how long they'd live. "Jordan, I have to tell you something. I can shift now."

His brows wrinkled together. "You can?"

Her cheeks heated, despite their current situation. "Yeah. It was something that happened while I was... with Jude."

A trickle of blood seeped from the corner of Jordan's mouth as he smiled. "Is there something between you and Jude?"

"Yeah. Well, I mean, there was. He told me everything he'd been feeling for me, and I'd been feeling it, too. Jordan, I wasn't sure if I would ever feel that. Even when I did, I doubted it. I didn't think I was good enough. I was so excited about it, but Jude doesn't want to have anything to do with me anymore."

"What did he do to you?" Jordan squirmed to straighten up, the smile on his face quickly turning to a scowl. "I'll kill him."

"That's exactly what he's afraid of. He said he didn't want to be with me because it would make you angry, and he refused to betray you. Then he rattled off some stuff about being an orphan and not belonging to a clan in the same way that I do and something about bloodlines, that he's not good enough for me. I don't know. I think it was just an excuse because I'm not like everyone else." She looked down at her lap, feeling ashamed all over again.

"It's probably not an excuse," Jordan replied quietly. "Jude and his brother were orphaned when they were really young, but I guess he told you that. He's been hung up on it ever since, because he doesn't believe he actually belongs anywhere. He told me on one of his visits home from the Army that he loved the brotherhood of it. There were times when his service was miserable, but he liked knowing he was a part of something. Knowing him, I wouldn't be surprised at all if he thinks he's not good enough for you."

"Really?"

Jordan nodded. "He's spent a lot of time distancing himself from anything that might make him happy, because he's too worried about it breaking his heart again. And he was always working so hard to be strong for Reid. Even as a kid, I could see how much he was hurting. When we get out of here, Annie, I'll sit down with him and have a long talk."

"So, you wouldn't be upset if he and I were together? I mean, not that I need your permission, but he seems to think we do." A small ball of excitement built up in her stomach, even though she didn't want to get her hopes up.

"Never." He leaned against her, the closest he could get to hugging her at the moment. "Annie, I know I've been protective of you. I've worried about you, and you shouldn't have had to feel the need to push back against me all the time. I want you to be safe and happy, but I'd never deny you of your fated destiny. If Jude is your one true mate, then so be it. At least it's someone I know and trust. Not like Austin. And I'm sorry about that whole thing."

"Don't worry about it. I don't blame you. You just wanted the best for me, and Austin pulled the wool over both our eyes." She hoped she'd get the chance to see just what it was like to dig her claws into his flesh before this was all over with.

"I wanted you to be happy, but that wasn't the only reason I was so weird about you finding someone." Jordan snuck a look at her from the corner of his eye. "When I took over the clan, Mom and Dad and some of our older relatives sat down with me. I figured it was just going to be one of those long boring talks about how important it was to be the Alpha, how it might be hard at first, and all that. There was some of that, but they also said there would be some very important shifters to come from our bloodline. I don't understand all of it, but they said there was this prophecy about one of our mates carrying the mark of the helix. Jude has it, doesn't he?"

Annie's mind was suddenly filled with the image of that silvery, swirly mark on Jude's chest. "Yeah."

"I thought so. It's been a long time since he and I were both in our bear forms together, and I hadn't even thought about that mark until I was told about this. I just kind of dismissed it, but it sounds to me like the two of you really are meant to be together."

"Wow." Annie already knew what she felt in her heart and soul for Jude. There was little that could convince her otherwise, and even his denial of how good they could be together wouldn't have kept them apart for long. She'd let her temper and heartache get the best of her.

"I'm happy for you, but I just hope you get the chance to tell him. I don't know what we're going to do." Jordan tipped his head back against the wall, mussing that hair that'd been the subject of countless articles in men's magazines.

"I'll tell you what we're going to do. We're going to shift and get the hell out of here." Annie had a true purpose in her life now. She had to get back to Jude, and if that meant going through Austin and the assholes who chose to follow him, then so be it.

"That's not going to work. I already told you. These things will cut right into my flesh if I shift, and they'll be far too tight."

"They will, but it's not like anything bad will happen immediately. Austin used these on you with the thought that you'd be down here by yourself. Bear teeth are pretty damn strong, so if I shift, I can tear enough of the metal to get you free. Then you can do the same for me. We'll tackle the door together." Now that she had a plan in mind, she couldn't wait to see it come to fruition.

"Shouldn't I be the one to shift first?" Jordan asked. "It's going to hurt."

Annie grinned at her big brother. "I'm smaller than you, so it won't hurt me as badly. Besides, I do all my own stunts." She turned away from him and closed her eyes, thinking about Jude and that night under the stars. Annie promised herself they'd find a chance to relive that night if she got out of this. She tapped into that feeling of wildness and freedom that came with her bear, happy to see it rise to the surface with much more ease this time. She moaned as her bear emerged and found itself in the same shackled position as her human, the ties cutting painfully into her. Annie knew she could do this.

9

———

Jude went straight to the coffee pot as soon as he got back to headquarters. There was something comforting about listening to the grinder decimating the beans and the pot steaming and bubbling away. It filled the kitchen with his favorite scent in the world—other than Annie.

Damn it. There'd be no getting away from her. He could tell her they would stay away from each other, and he could keep his distance from her as much as possible while they searched for Jordan, but she would always be there in the back of his mind and the depths of his heart. Their distance over the passing years had made his wonderment about her subside, but now that his beast had claimed her, there was no turning back.

To make matters worse, he felt like a complete asshole for letting her down the way he had. Annie needed him. Logically, though, Jude knew it'd been the right decision. The hard ones usually didn't feel good.

"There he is, finally back from his little Sin City trip! How'd it go, bro?"

Jude had just pulled a mug down from the cabinet, but he turned to find Reid standing just behind him. A woman was at his side, short and diminutive with skin like porcelain. Her ebony hair was streaked with traces of auburn, and her dark eyes had a look to them that said she'd be glad to kick ass and take names if she needed to. Jude liked her instantly. "You must be Mali. I'm sorry you got stuck with the likes of my brother."

She smiled sweetly up at Reid and laughed. "If it's my burden, then I'm willing to bear it."

"Hey!" Reid protested, but he planted a kiss on her neck. "Mali, this is my brother, Jude. Jude, this is Mali."

"Since you're here, can I assume you've decided to stay on with the Force?" Jude filled his mug to the brim and sipped some of the hot, bitter liquid from the top. Perfection.

"I tried to call you about that, actually, but you

haven't been answering your phone," Reid pointed out.

"Oh, right. Sorry." Jude had seen a missed call, but he'd been too preoccupied with Annie to worry about it. His brother would always be there, and Annie... well, Annie was a different story altogether. "I've been a little preoccupied with my mission."

"Does that mean it went well, or did it go to shit?"

"Before I start answering your questions, you need to answer mine. Are you staying?" Jude took another sip, using the motion to hide the fact that he was holding his breath.

"Yeah." Reid gave another lovey-dovey look to Mali. "It's going to be the best for both of us here. Besides, you won't have any excuses to bail on our wedding."

"Congratulations, guys." Jude shook each of their hands. Not all destined mates chose to take that extra step, but he was truly happy for Reid. "That's great news."

"Thank you. Now that you know it's official, tell me about Vegas."

Jude glanced at Mali. He had no doubts about her, considering she and Reid were meant to be together, but some things could only be discussed among brothers.

Fortunately, she seemed to get the hint. "I have a little more unpacking to do, if you gentlemen will excuse me."

Reid watched her backside as she glided from the kitchen. "She's something else, man. I can't believe how lucky I am. It's the sort of thing that makes me wish everyone would find their mates."

"I don't know. What if you find the one, but it's impossible for the two of you to be together? Surely, that has to happen now and then." Jude frowned down into his cup, finding no solace in the dark brew.

"Okay, sounds like you have plenty to talk about. I think I'll make myself comfortable." Reid turned for the fridge, pulled out a cold cut and cheese platter, and sat down at the bar with it. "I'm all ears."

"Do yourself a favor and keep Mali out of any missions you might go on," Jude advised. "No offense to her, she seems like a great girl. But it makes things so much more complicated. It's enough to think about keeping yourself and the other Force members safe while accomplishing your task. Women just add a whole new layer of trouble."

"Jude," Reid warned, "you're beating around the

bush. It's not going to have any leaves left on it by the time you're done."

"Okay. What really happened, if I were to write up a report about it, is that Jordan's stunt double drugged and kidnapped him in order to take over his career. Someone else came in and bought Jordan off of him, and we have no idea who it was or why they would do such a thing. They knew he was a shifter, though, so there's definitely something crazy going on."

"That's fucking wild," Reid admitted, sandwiching a piece of cheese between two hunks of salami. "What's the redacted part?"

"Having Annie next to me on the plane, in the car, in the hotel room next to mine, and fighting alongside me. I know I felt something for her a long time ago, but enough time had gone by that I thought I must have been wrong. I was determined to remain professional, but then she opened up to me and told me one of her deepest, darkest secrets. And I repaid the favor by blabbing about how I felt about her." Just retelling it made him feel a little nuts.

Reid squinted painfully. "And she didn't feel the same way?"

"She did, actually! She told me she was feeling

the exact same thing. We hooked up under the stars, Reid, and it was the most incredible thing I'd ever experienced in my goddamn life!" Jude slammed his fist down onto the countertop.

"I know you pretty well, Jude, but this isn't making sense. What exactly is the problem?"

Sinking onto one of the barstools, Jude leaned his elbows heavily on the counter. "She's Jordan's sister. I can't possibly be with her. It would ruin everything between my best friend and me."

Reid raised an eyebrow. "Dude, you sound like me before I met Mali."

"What does that mean?"

"You know exactly what it means." Reid punched him gently in the arm. "I didn't want to be tied down, and I would've made any excuse not to be. I would've made up some story that sounded good enough inside my head, but once I said it out loud, everyone would know it was complete shit."

"It's not shit," Jude argued. "There's a lot going on for the two of us. Besides, Annie is second-in-command of her clan right now. If we don't find Jordan, she's going to become Alpha. It wouldn't make any sense for her to be dealing with all that, and for me to be working with the Force. We'd never see each other. What?"

Reid was leveling the most serious look Jude had ever seen on his face. "That's pretty much the same things. It's just another way to justify what you're doing, even though it's completely wrong."

"Like you'd know," Jude sneered, feeling bitter at the world.

"Go ahead and be mad at me if it makes you feel better, Jude. I'm not worried about it, because I know eventually, you're going to figure out how you're sabotaging yourself. Just do me a favor and think about this: it's one thing to screw yourself over if you're the only one who's going to suffer. It's completely different if it affects someone else." Reid covered the plate and got up to put it back in the fridge.

"I'm not screwing anyone. If anything, I'm making the decision that's best for everyone, even if it's not best for me. I'd say that's pretty generous." Jude knew he was making himself miserable, but Annie would have a better chance of happiness with someone else. In the back of his mind, he was also holding onto the idea that Annie was too good for him. Reid wouldn't want to hear that, but it was true.

"Oh, you're such a friggin' martyr," Reid cracked. "Who says it's up to you, anyway? I mean, when Mali and I met, it was a completely mutual thing."

"You've known her for how long? And you're already acting like you're the expert on fated mates," Jude derided. "I don't need Professor Reid to lecture me on the ways of the heart."

"I think you do. You're hiding behind your excuses, and you're acting as though this is all up to you. Annie is a grown woman, and she can decide for herself. Hell, the universe has already told you how things are supposed to be. Who are you to argue?"

Jude's lips tightened. He had no retort for that. Reid was right. "Fine. I'll give you a point for that one. But even so, how am I supposed to get around the Jordan problem? He was always so concerned about who Annie ended up with."

"Since you don't even know where he is, I wouldn't worry about it for now. Drive over there, scoop her into your arms, and tell her you can't live without her. Spend all day in bed together, banging from sunrise to sunset, and then decide if you really care about what Jordan says." Reid softly stared through the living room toward the staircase, no doubt thinking of Mali.

"You're right, but you're also love drunk. I don't know. Maybe she and I should sit down and talk it over, but not right now. I've got to find Jordan first. Everything else has to wait."

"Fair enough," Reid conceded. "In the meantime, I think I might take my own suggestion." He moved toward the stairs.

Just then, Raul came in from the conference room. "Jude! I'm glad you're here. I was just about to call you. I found some intel on the Jeep."

"Awesome. Where do I need to go?" He was more than ready to run back to Vegas or anywhere else as long as it kept him far away from Annie.

"About twenty minutes away," Raul said solemnly. "Just knowing it was a black Jeep wasn't much to go on, but I was able to tap into enough surveillance cameras that I found the one that'd been at Evan Boyer's house. A few more tries and I got a plate number, but you're not going to like where I traced it back to."

"Just tell me," Jude urged. "Jordan's probably in serious danger."

Raul sighed and set his laptop on the counter. "Right here. It's Annie's clubhouse. The Jeep belongs to a guy named Austin Reed."

"Shit." Jude easily remembered the guy who'd come out to the gazebo to confront them when he'd gone to visit Annie. "This was an inside job. I thought because the stunt double was involved—who's not a shifter, by the way—that it was something entirely human."

"At least you don't have to worry about the word getting out about us," Reid pointed out, having stuck around to find out what was going on instead of following Mali upstairs.

"Except that I just dropped Annie off at that exact address," Jude replied. "I've got to go."

Reid nodded. "I'm coming with you."

"I'll round up the others, and we'll be on your heels," Raul promised, shutting his laptop with a click and heading off into the house.

———

"HERE WE GO." JUDE PULLED TO A HALT ONCE AGAIN in front of Annie's house. "We've got to do this right, Reid. I don't know how many clan members are working against the Martinezes, or even if Annie is still here." A wave of nausea washed over him as he imagined all the harm that could've befallen her in the short time since he'd dropped her off.

"It'll be all right," Reid assured him, smiling slightly. "I'm glad to be on my first official Force mission with my brother, and I can't think of a better way of welcoming Annie to the family than by rescuing her."

Jude glanced at his brother. "You have to take this seriously," he warned. "This isn't just some stupid mission where you can act like a hotshot and not worry about the consequences."

"The only reason I'm not going to take that as an insult is because I would've done something just like that only a few years ago. Despite what my military records might say, things are different now." He got out and shut the door behind him. "I'm on this."

Checking his phone, Jude nodded. "I've got the confirmation from Raul. They're heading in through the back, so we've got the place covered. Let's go."

He strode up to the door as though he were just coming back to return an item Annie had left behind. In fact, that was the exact excuse Jude had cooked up as they'd prepared to leave the house, and he was ready with it when a man answered the door with a scowl.

"What do you want?"

"I'd like to see Annie, please," Jude said with a pleasant smile.

"Who are you?"

"Just a friend. She accidentally left her jacket in my car, and I'd like to return it." The jacket he had draped over his elbow was actually Emersyn's, and it'd been conveniently on a hook near the door.

"I'll take it to her," the man offered. He had shaved his head, which revealed a thick, ropy scar that wound back from his forehead and around his ear.

Jude had to wonder what kind of accident would make a wound like that. "I'd rather deliver it to her myself, actually." Without waiting for an invitation, Jude pushed past the man and into the living room.

"You can't just come in here!" he protested, but now Reid and Jude were both in the room. "Just leave the jacket and go."

"I wouldn't want to put the burden on you," Jude explained, still keeping that calm demeanor as he surveyed the room. There was no evidence of a struggle in there, but Annie's suitcase stood in the corner. Knowing what a stickler she was for checking every box and tying up every loose end, Jude doubted she'd have come home and just left it there.

"Fine. Have it your way." The man slammed the door behind them and swaggered up to Jude, his fists curled at his sides, and swung a meaty hand at Jude's head.

Jude easily dodged it. "There's no need for violence. Just fetch Annie for me, please."

The bald guy swung again, lower this time.

Jude swerved backward. "I can tell that you're either a little hard of hearing or a little slow. I'm not here to fight. I'm just here to see Annie."

Reid snickered, bringing the bald man's attention.

"Oh, yeah? You think this is funny, asshole?" Growling, he went for Reid.

It was just the distraction Jude needed, and he saw the glint of mischief in his brother's eyes. Reid had this. Jude headed through the doorway and into the kitchen. No one was there, and he continued into the hallway just as a door opened to his left.

"Dominic! What's going on up here? I told you to answer the door and get rid of whoever it was!" Because of the direction the door opened, the man didn't see Jude right away. But as soon as he slammed it behind him, Jude recognized Austin.

"*You*," the blonde man said, narrowing his eyes. "What the hell do you want?"

"I'm here to talk to Annie, and I'm tired of repeating myself." Jude assessed his opponent. Austin was a big guy with plenty of muscles, but he didn't have the look of a trained fighter. Behind him,

Jude could hear choking sounds coming from the man who must have been Dominic.

Austin nodded. "I see. You come sniffing around here once or twice and think you have some sort of right to her. Well, Annie told me she never wants to see you again."

"I want to hear it straight from her mouth," Jude challenged.

"No," Austin thundered. "In fact, she's chosen me as her mate, which gives me the authority to speak for her."

Jude knew it wasn't true. Annie didn't want to have anything to do with this thug, but the very idea of it sent a fire of rage and jealousy through his blood. "I want to hear it from *her*," he hissed.

"Intruders!" Austin shouted before charging down the hall toward Jude.

Jude was ready, and he blocked the first blow. It reverberated in his bones, but already he had that urge to protect Annie. He shoved Austin back with his elbow, knocking him against the wall. Before he could gain his balance, Jude snagged the front of his shirt and slammed him into the wall once again. "Tell me where she is, right now!"

"Fuck off!" Austin kicked out with one foot, bending Jude's knee backward.

Pain flooded his vision with swirling colors, but it reached deep inside him and pulled out his best weapon. His knee popped back into place as his leg thickened and shortened, the effect rippling up his back and tickling the underside of his scalp as he shifted into his bear form.

Austin had done the same, and now there were two bears in the hallway with very little room to maneuver. There was no place to go but forward, and his ursine mouth didn't allow Jude to ask any further questions. He attacked, shoving the other bear backward as he bared his teeth and slashed his paws through the air. The two of them tumbled through the narrow space, spilling out into a conference room.

Jude roared his rage and anger, finding that same fury inside him back at that little house on the outskirts of Vegas. Annie was in trouble, and he would stop at nothing to save her.

Austin had the advantage of knowing the room, and he thrust Jude toward the table. He caught himself as he crashed into a rolling chair that sped off across the room, knowing the full weight of Austin's attack was coming swiftly on his heels. The other bear fought with no style, but he was strong.

Jude felt the edge of the table making a hard line

against his back as Austin roared in his face, and he swiped his claws toward the other beast. The house had erupted with crashing and shouting, and Jude knew the rest of the SOS Force had arrived. A second, deep black bear showed up through the door of the conference room, but Jude didn't recognize him. Now it was two against one.

Driving his paw forward with all his might, Jude sank his claws into Austin's side. The bear moaned in agony, his hot breath a cloud in Jude's face. With his claws still in the other man's flesh, Jude shoved him hard to the side. He needed to use all the inertia he could get, and he charged down the line of chairs until he slammed Austin's giant head into the flat-screen television mounted on the wall. Blood spurted through Austin's fur, and he sank to the floor.

Jude could already feel the other bear coming after him. He didn't have much time. Just as he turned, a wolf crashed through the window, who Jude instantly recognized as Raul.

I've got this one. Raul bared his teeth as he bounced off a chair and leapt onto the table, crashing down onto the back of the darker bear's neck. *Find Annie.*

How's everyone else? Jude sent the message out to

the rest of the Force, not knowing who had shifted yet. Through ancient dragon magic, they shared a telepathic link that was typically reserved only for mates or those in a true clan, not one that'd been pieced together like the Force.

Reid, who hadn't yet been inducted into the Force with their official ceremony, still had a brotherly bond with Jude that allowed him to speak. *There are a lot of these bastards. I just took out two in the living room, but I think more are coming.*

I just came in through the kitchen door. It was Gabe, which meant there were now three Force members who were there fighting as bears. *Emersyn is at her clinic, and Amar is out on recon. No dragons or panthers for us today.*

I'm glad you're here. I'm heading downstairs. Though Jude didn't like to pin himself into any sort of corner, there had to be some reason Austin was in the basement earlier.

I've got your six, Reid replied.

It would've been handy to be in his human form to navigate the door handle, but Jude didn't want to waste time. He crashed against it with his shoulder, splintering the area near the latch. One more hard ram and it was off its hinges, hanging sadly through the opening to the stairwell.

Jude charged down, immediately confronted by two more of Austin's men in bear form. Like him, they weren't trained fighters. They lunged forward, both attacking at once and hardly giving each other enough room to swing their arms. As they came straight for Jude, he picked the one on the left and charged as well. His teeth sank into the thick flesh of the bear's neck. Jude clamped down harder, ignoring the blows that were hitting his back.

I've got him! Reid called out.

The other bear was no longer hitting Jude, and a heavy crash sounded as the two bears went tumbling away into the corner.

Blood filled his mouth, and he let go just long enough to get another good hold. His would-be attacker bellowed in pain as he flailed uselessly at Jude's back. One claw made it through Jude's thick fur, and he felt the burn of blood as it welled to the surface. Jude wasn't playing around. He clenched his teeth as hard as a vice and yanked his head to the right, ripping out the other bear's throat. His enemy fell to the floor, twitching.

"Very good," a familiar human voice said.

Jude turned to see Austin coming down the stairs. Blood ran down the side of his head, the wound mostly closed due to the inherent healing powers of shifters. He grinned as he staggered off the bottom step, puffing out his chest, full of just as much arrogance as ever. He clapped slowly as he came to stand in front of Jude. "What's the matter? You can't face me like a man?"

Jude knew better than to fall for that. He would be vulnerable while in the middle of his shift, and he wasn't going to give Austin the least bit of an advantage. It stopped Jude from saying all the things he wanted to the asshole, and that was the only thing that tempted him.

Austin glared at him, his anger simmering clearly just under the surface. "You and your friends can come and fight, but you'll never win. There are far more clan members here who want me to be their Alpha, and we'll get our way. You might as well tuck your stumpy little tail between your legs and head on back to wherever the hell you came from, because you're on *my* territory now."

Just then, a door on the side of the room crashed open. Two bears charged through it. Jude instantly recognized Jordan, with his dark coat and broad shoulders. Annie was next to him, the gold flecks in her fur sparkling brilliantly despite the poor lighting. Brother and sister attacked in unison, taking Austin down forever.

10

ANNIE SLOWLY STOOD, TRYING TO REGAIN HER BALANCE after shifting so quickly back into her human form. Everything had happened so fast, and it was going to take some time before she could catch up to the rest of them.

But seeing Jude just across the room was all the motivation she needed. Annie swiped a self-conscious hand through her hair as she stumbled to him and pulled him into a kiss. It was pure instinct. She didn't know if he'd push her away, but she was rewarded with the warm embrace of his arms around her back, pulling her in tightly as he deepened the kiss.

"I'm so glad you're here," she whispered against his lips, still clinging tightly to him.

"Of course I am," he said. His eyes skidded to the side and his cheeks reddened. "Um, your brother's here, too."

"I'm afraid you're the only one who cares about that," Jordan said, clapping his old friend on the shoulder. "Annie and I had some quality time together stuck in that closet, and she told me about your concerns."

Now it was Annie's turn to have her cheeks redden. She didn't want Jude to think she was talking about him behind his back. Most of the time, Annie didn't worry too much about what people thought about her. Like everything else with Jude, this was different. "I didn't know if we'd ever get out of there."

"It's all right," Jude said, pulling back a little and squeezing her hand. "There's no point in keeping it a secret."

"Especially for such a dumb reason," Jordan said playfully. "Dude, I couldn't possibly be mad at finding out the two of you are mates. You're one of the people I trust the most in the world."

Jude was the one who needed convincing, but hearing Annie's brother say this to him still made her feel better. That didn't take care of all their problems, though. "Jude, if there's some other reason you don't want to be with me, then please just tell me now." Her lungs froze in her chest as she gazed into those deep green eyes of his.

"Hold up," Jordan interrupted. "There might be more that the two of you need to hash out later, but I've got something I need to tell you, Jude."

Jude glanced at Annie and then back at his friend, hearing the serious tone in Jordan's voice. "What is it?"

The actor stuffed his hands in his pockets. "When this clan was handed down to me, I was told that someone in our bloodline would be fated to a bear who bore the mark of the helix. I didn't know anything about that when we were younger, but now, there's no doubt in my mind that it's you."

"The mark of the—" Jude touched his chest. "Oh. What does that mean?"

"Beats me," Jordan replied honestly. "We can talk about it later. I'm going to go make sure the rest of the house is secured. It's going to be interesting to sort out who's who. I never expected my own clan to revolt against me."

"I've got a man up there. I'm coming with you." Jude took Annie's hand and headed for the stairs. "I have to tell you, I was pretty impressed to see you take Austin down like that."

Her cheeks flushed again, but for a different reason this time. "What can I say? I learned from the best."

"You definitely didn't learn that from me," Jude argued, keeping her at his side as they made their way upstairs. "That was all right there inside you. I just helped you find it."

She knew she should've been happy. They'd found Jordan and took down Austin. They still had a few things to take care of, but everything was going to be okay. Still, Annie didn't know where she truly stood with Jude. He'd come to her rescue, but that didn't mean anything. "Jude, if we need to find time to talk about it later, then we can, but I really want to know where we stand." She didn't like thinking they were just going to go on with their lives without getting down to an answer.

He paused as they reached the upstairs hallway. "The truth is, I've been a complete idiot. I guess I was afraid that if I let myself love you, it was going to fall apart just like everything else in my life. I'm absolutely crazy about you, and if you can forgive me for being such a jackass, then I want to be with you for the rest of our lives."

Heat flooded her body as he held her close. "I do forgive you, but only if you can forgive me."

"You? What am I supposed to forgive you for?" Jude took her hand once again as they headed toward the living room.

"I know I'm not perfect. I can be too uptight, and sometimes I take things more seriously than they need to be." It was something she'd started thinking a lot about since that magical night in Red Rock Canyon, and it was something she wanted to change.

"I think I can handle that," Jude replied. "Besides, if it weren't for you taking things so seriously, none of this would've turned out the way it did."

A FIRE CRACKLED IN THE CENTER OF THE CLEARING. Annie walked through the dark trees, keeping her eyes focused on the light ahead of them. "Are you sure this is what you want to do?"

Jordan walked along beside her, his head held high. "There's not a doubt in my mind."

That was great, but there were still plenty of doubts in *her* mind. "You were the one who was chosen for the position," she countered. "I don't know if it's a good idea to mess that up. When I came to you about problems within the clan, I never meant that you should step down as Alpha."

"I don't see it as stepping down," Jordan said. "I'm not just quitting because I have other things I want to do. I'm doing my job as Alpha by making sure that the clan is taken care of by the best person for the job. That's you, Annie. It always has been, and I'm pissed at myself for not seeing it before now."

"I didn't do anything."

"You did." Jordan stopped and took her by the shoulders, turning her so that she faced him. His face had been shaven clean, and the wounds he'd endured had healed over nicely. He'd informed his producer that he was ill and had to take a short hiatus from shooting, but he'd be back on the set within a few days. "You knew something was wrong, and you came to me. When that didn't work, you went to someone else who could help. If it weren't for you and Jude, I'd be dead right now. The rest of our clan would either be dead or wish they were. Annie, you've always taken better care of this family than I have. You deserve this, and everyone knows it. It might've been my idea to do this, but everyone else agreed."

She nodded, glad to know everyone was on board. "I guess let's get this part over with, then."

A drum sounded, cueing Jordan to enter the clearing. Annie stood back and watched as he marched to the fire in the center, bending to take a blazing torch from the pile of wood. He held it high over his head.

"The clan recognizes the Alpha, he who watches over us all," intoned the elderly voice of their Uncle Glen.

The gathering of bears murmured their assent, and another drumbeat sounded.

Annie pulled in a breath and followed her brother's path. She kept her eyes focused on him as she entered the circle, keenly aware of the rest of the clan's eyes on her. Their number had been pared down significantly now that Austin and his cohorts had been removed. Even so, plenty had come out to see this unprecedented event.

"The clan recognizes the beta," Uncle Glen announced.

Coming up next to Jordan, Annie stopped and stood with her shoulder nearly rubbing his arm. Her stomach roiled inside her, but then she caught a glimpse of Jude standing just outside the edge of the firelight. He smiled at her, and once again, she knew everything was going to be all right.

Jordan held the torch high. "I've been your Alpha for five years now," he said. "I thank the clan for everything it has done for me, but I recognize that I haven't done enough for it. For *you*. We are a gathering of some of the greatest bear shifters to exist, and you deserve the very best. This is why, with your permission, I pass this torch and the position of Alpha to my sister, Annie Martinez." He lowered the flaming piece of wood and held it in front of her.

Annie swallowed. The procedure was simple enough. There was no reason for it not to go well. Jordan had assured her that this was what everyone wanted, including him. Even if there were some bears among their ranks who still weren't certain about her, they wouldn't dare go against what he wanted. Would they?

She took the torch, the wood rough on her hands, and the fire warm on her face. She stared into the flame for a moment before hoisting it as high over her head as possible. The gathered shifters erupted with cheers and applause, showing her their approval.

It was Uncle Glen's turn again. "We recognize

and welcome our new Alpha!" he announced, eliciting even more accolades from the crowd.

Annie waited patiently for the noise to die down. "Thank you. I will guide the clan for my entire life, and I will listen to the guidance of my elders." She placed the torch back on the fire to represent her oneness with the clan.

After more applause, the ceremony turned to a bonfire party. Food and drinks were brought out, and everyone took the chance to catch up with each other.

Jude handed her a glass of wine. "You were spectacular."

"If you say so. That was actually a little embarrassing." She didn't like having all those eyes on her, though she knew it wouldn't be the last time. Everyone would be watching her first actions as Alpha.

"At least it's over. I'm hoping that means the two of us can find a little time to be alone together." He raised one eyebrow, the fire reflecting in his gaze.

Someone cleared their throat, and Annie turned to find Uncle Glen standing nearby. "I wanted a chance to speak with you."

Jude stepped back. "I'll be over here with Jordan."

"No, I want to talk to you, too," Glen corrected. "I understand you carry the sign of the helix."

A troubled look passed over Jude's face, but he quickly cleared it away. "Yes. Jordan and I were just discussing that last week."

Glen put a hand on Jude's shoulder. "I want to apologize to you. I didn't realize any of this until Jordan told me about it, and if I had, I would have told you a long time ago. You might not remember me, but I was around sometimes when you used to come to the clubhouse."

"What is it?"

"Jude, I know you were orphaned when you were very young. What you might not realize is that the symbol on your chest is a sign of very prominent lineage from a very old clan, one that was unfortunately decimated the night that your parents were killed."

Annie watched the exchange with interest, though she felt for Jude. It couldn't be easy for him to bring all those memories to the surface.

"I never knew much about that night," he replied honestly. "We were young, and the Hoffmans never wanted to talk about it."

Uncle Glen nodded. "That's understandable. It was tragic. You see, your original clan was at war with another that was trying to take over their territory. They lost their final battle that night, but you and your brother were lucky enough to have been at the Hoffmans'. Our clan, your parents' clan, and the Hoffmans' had all been friendly with each other for a long time, which is why I know anything about this at all."

Jude glanced down at the ground. "I see. At least they died nobly, fighting for what they believed in. Our foster parents just told us it was an accident."

Annie slipped her hand into his. She didn't want this night to be marred by such terrible news, but it needed to be out there.

"I'm sure they were just trying to protect you," Glen replied. "Your father was the Alpha of his clan. He had that same mark on his chest, as it only ever showed on the first-born. You are a descendent of great nobility, Jude. Do with that what you will, but know that we're delighted to have you as part of our family." He clapped Jude on the shoulder once again, gave them a nod, and moved off to mingle.

"Are you all right?" Annie asked. Jude was always so stoic on the outside. It made him hard to read, but she was working on it.

He turned to her and smiled. "Actually, yeah."

"I would've thought you'd be upset hearing all that."

He put an arm around her and pulled her close. "No. I miss my parents, but that's a very old wound. It's not going to go away, but it can't really get worse. Knowing they were fighting for something they believed in makes me proud. If I'm honest, I can't say it hurts to know the truth about where they stood in their clan and what that patch of fur means. Now I know I'm good enough for you." He kissed her on the forehead.

Annie leaned into his embrace. "What are you talking about? You've always been good enough for me."

"You can say that, but now I know it." He trailed his kisses down her nose and to her mouth, ignoring the large number of people who'd gathered there for the ceremony. "So, Alpha Annie, what are you doing after this?"

"You, if I'm lucky," she teased.

They joined the festivities, eating and drinking and celebrating with the clan. The two of them ended up slipping away and heading back to the clubhouse while the fire was still burning brightly.

"I don't want you to miss out on any of the ceremony," Jude said as they headed inside. "I know this is a special night for you."

"Then you can help me make it extra special," she replied, grabbing his hand and leading him up the stairs to her room. The ceremony in the woods and the clan's acceptance of her had brought out something inside her, and Jude brought out even more. She felt every cell of her body tingling with life, and she didn't want to waste it.

Jude grinned. "I think I can help you with that." He shut the door behind him and grabbed her by the waist, yanking her into his arms and pressing his mouth against hers. He was already hard against her, which only made Annie all the more eager for him.

She kissed him back, scrunching her hands through his thick hair and down his neck. Her body surged toward him, hungry for all she knew he could give her. She felt her need for him in the very marrow of her bones as she pulled off his shirt and tossed it aside, pressing herself against his bare skin.

Jude growled softly as he scraped his teeth across the side of her neck. His big hands moved under her shirt, his thumbs brushing her pert nipples through the satin material of her bra. She lifted her shirt over her head to assist him, feeling her core tighten as he brushed his lips over the tips of each mound.

"How long is it going to be before anyone else gets back here?" has asked as he unbuttoned her jeans and sank his fingertips down between the denim and her thighs, touching the entire length of each leg as he removed them. "There are so many things I want to do to you tonight."

"I'm sure we'll have time for at least some of them, and then you can save the rest for tomorrow, and the night after that, and the night after that." Annie was down to her bra and panties now, and she was eager for him to catch up. She stripped away the rest of his clothing so that his hardness brushed against the thin layer of fabric that still separated them from each other.

He was absolutely gorgeous in either form he was in, but at the moment, Annie found herself particularly appreciative of this one. His broad chest and chiseled abs were just the beginning. The way he held her, the way they fit together at their most intimate moments when their souls reached outside their bodies to touch one another was the most attractive thing she could imagine. "I want you to know how much I appreciate you," she said as she dropped to her knees in front of him.

"You don't have to do that to let me know—oh."

Jude's head thumped against the wall as it rolled back, and his hands tangled in her hair.

"I want to," she murmured, kissing and licking down the length of him. "Besides, it turns me on."

"If you insist," he panted, his hands hardening into fists as he tried to control himself.

Annie had felt a tremor of electricity starting at her core as they'd come into the room, and now it cascaded into waves of excitement that drove her on as she pleasured him. Hearing his moans and knowing how much he was enjoying it made her want to do this all night.

His knees were shaking by the time she finally pulled back. She took his hand and brought him to the bed, thinking they would get down to business.

But Jude had a different idea. He grabbed her by the waist, his strength fanning the fire of her infatuation as he flipped her onto her back. He mounted the bed so that he was on top of her, bracing himself on all fours and grinning down at her. "You can't possibly think you can be so good to me and not get anything in return."

He kissed his way down her neck, along her collarbone, and down the delicate skin of her side. He clung to her tightly as his tongue made slow, lazy circles around each nipple, sucking each one of them into the hot wetness of his mouth and leaving them cold and longing when he was done. His lips worked down the plateau of her stomach, and he surprised her by skipping down to her inner thigh and making his way down her legs.

Jude's hands took over the work by the time he reached her legs, and he massaged his way back up her body. His fingers were warm and knowing, finding even the tiniest of aches in her body and working them out slowly, never rushing. He was so patient, even though she lay spread out and ready before him.

"Turn over," he murmured.

She did as she was told, not wanting this incredible feeling to stop. It felt physically good to have his fingers brush her hair aside, rubbing her shoulders and moving further down her back, but there was so much more to it than that. Jude cared for her. He wasn't just there to get what he needed and go. He appreciated her like no other man in her life ever had, and she felt it in the way he squeezed and rubbed her.

"Did I put you to sleep?" he asked as he pressed his palms into her backside.

"No, but I think I've melted inside," she said with a smile.

"Turn over again. I think I missed a spot." Jude moved further down the bed between her legs, flicking his tongue against her sensitive bud. He was hot and wet against her, and after that impromptu massage, Annie had no choice but to relax into the feeling. His tongue worked against her, twirling against her soft, aching flesh until her thighs were quaking and her hips bucked against him. Pressing two thick fingers inside her, he rhythmically pressed against her G-spot, and within seconds, her inner walls began to contract, every muscle rippling in perfect synchronization as she reached her peak.

But he didn't stop there. Jude pulled her to the edge of the bed and took her from behind, his cock sliding into her as his hands gripped her hips. As his right hand slipped between her legs, his fingertips began massaging slick circles over her clit.

"I want you to come as many times as possible," he said, bringing his left hand up to cup her breast as he dragged his tongue along her back.

She couldn't resist the magic he worked on her, and Annie was grateful there was no one else in the house as she screamed her pleasure twice more. Annie turned over beneath him, once again rejoicing in the way he filled her. She wrapped her legs around him as his hips thrust against hers, and before she knew it, she was being pushed over that edge yet again as Jude buried his face in her shoulder and growled with his release.

Annie fought to catch her breath as they lay next to each other, too hot to bother getting under the covers. "I'm glad we did this tonight."

"You don't think you're missing out on anything happening in the woods?" Jude tucked her against his side and held her tightly.

"There's nothing I'd rather do than this. Besides, if we get our own place like we talked about, then this could be our only chance to have fun in this room." She snuggled in against him, feeling how calm her bear was inside. Never in her life had it been so much at peace.

He kissed her forehead. "I think that'll be a good idea. I actually saw a place online that I think might work. We can go look at it tomorrow if you want."

"Grab your phone and show me the pictures. Maybe we could drive by it tonight." Until they'd started talking about it, Annie hadn't realized just how much she'd wanted a change, and getting out of that house she'd been living in her entire life was the perfect start.

"Nope." He sank further down into the mattress.

"No? But I'm excited about it."

He grinned as he tangled his legs with hers. "So am I, but I've got other plans for tonight."

Her protests were drowned as he kissed her, and Annie realized he was right.

Everything else could wait.

THE END

REID

Reid stepped out of the backyard at the Special Ops Shifter Force L.A. headquarters, leaving behind all the lanterns, tablecloths, and the chink of champagne glasses to catch a moment of peace. He spotted a familiar figure in the kitchen, and he stepped up quietly behind her before wrapping his arms around her waist and pulling her in tightly. "Hello there, Mrs. Sutton."

Mali giggled as she put down her glass and leaned back into him. "Unhand me you big monster! I've just gotten married, and I haven't even had a chance to share my husband's bed with him yet." She tipped up her face to kiss him.

"I certainly wouldn't want to mess that up. I happen to know your groom, and he's rather eager to get his life started with you." Reid turned her around in his arms and nuzzled her neck.

"We should get back outside," she said even as she tipped her head to the side to expose her throat. "It is our party, after all."

After pressing his lips against the warmth of hers once again, Reid pulled back and looked down at her. She was beautiful, both inside and out. Anyone could claim they'd met by sheer chance, but Reid knew better. The universe had brought them together, just as they were meant to be. "I can't believe we were able to fit so many of our friends and family in that backyard."

"Not all of them," she said with a frown. "I wish my family would've been able to come over from Thailand."

Reid pressed his forehead against hers, knowing how difficult it'd been for her to come to a new country and start all over again. "We'll find a way to get them here, and then we can get married all over again."

She gave him a playful smack on the arm. "You don't mean that."

"Yes, I do. I'll marry you as many times as I need to."

She thanked him with a deep kiss, and her eyes

were suggestive when she pulled back. "I'm going to get my things and go to the hotel."

"Okay. Let me just say goodbye and I'll be right behind you." Reid knew the pleasure of lying next to her in bed, their naked bodies sharing their heat, but there was something even more exciting about doing that on their wedding night.

"No." She put a finger on his chest, stopping him with the lightest touch. "I have a little surprise planned for you. Stay here and enjoy your family a little longer. You'll know where to find me."

He watched her head off to the bedroom they would be sharing there at HQ, wondering if he should've insisted that they spend their wedding night there. Reid didn't want to wait any longer than he had to. Still, it would be nice not to worry about everyone else around them as they officially started their lives together.

A hand clamped down on his shoulder. It was Jude. "Congratulations, little brother. It was a beautiful ceremony."

"I couldn't agree more, but I think I'm ready for it to be over with."

"And disappoint all the people out there?" Jude gestured toward the back of the house, where the retractable wall had been pulled back to make the party space flow easily between the house and the yard. The night was a beautiful one, and everyone was enjoying it under the stars.

"I've got more important things to take care of," Reid replied with a smirk. "You'd know more about that if you put a ring on Annie's finger."

"Hey, now. We've only just recently found each other. She's had to spend almost her whole life being responsible and doing what everyone else wants. I'd like to give her some time." Jude put his hands in his pockets and looked down at the floor.

Reid couldn't remember ever seeing his brother look so shy. "Annie's had a good effect on you. I'm glad you found her."

"Me, too. She's really something else, and it sounds like she and Mali are getting along well. The four of us should go out together sometime. You know, once you two get past the honeymoon stage and you can tear your eyes away from each other long enough to know what's going on around you," Jude joked.

"Yeah, yeah. Like you're not just as lovesick. I'm going to make the rounds, and then I'm taking off."

After receiving several more congratulations and making excuses for Mali's absence, Reid trotted out to the garage and headed across town. He hadn't been in L.A. very long, having just joined the Force. Already, he knew he was going to like it. There was always something happening, and now he had Mali to help him explore it. Reid let out a contented sigh as he thought about how much his life had changed. He never thought he'd settle down, and now he was happy to do so. Mali had made a huge difference in his life.

To save time, he and Mali had checked into their hotel earlier in the day. Reid hadn't wanted to waste time after the ceremony, and he was glad he had the keycard in his pocket as he took the elevator up the stairs. If he had it his way, they wouldn't get out of bed for the rest of the weekend. Considering she'd said she had a surprise for him, she was probably thinking the same.

The first surprise was in finding the hotel room door shut but not latched. He pushed it open warily, glancing down the hall to see if she'd stepped out to get some ice. "Mali?"

The overhead lights had been turned off, the room illuminated only by the candles that had been lit on every surface surrounding the massive bed. A tray of chocolate-covered strawberries sat next to an ice bucket and a bottle of champagne. She'd gone all out, and Reid couldn't say he minded being romanced a little.

"Mali?" He moved through the suite, wondering where she'd gone. When he pushed the bathroom door open, he saw her suitcase on the floor. It'd fallen over, her clothes spilling out onto the shining marble. Reid's heart raced. She'd been there, but now she was gone.

As he straightened, he noticed a smear of blood on the corner of the bathroom sink. Reid's bear went wild inside him. The instinct to protect his mate was a strong one, and something had definitely happened to her. He rushed back out of the bath-room to search the room for more clues, pulling his phone out of his pocket as he did.

"Jude, I need your help. Mali's missing."

———

Werebears of Acadia Series

Werebears of the Everglades Series

Werebears of Glacier Bay Series

Werebears of Big Bend Series

Dragons of Charok Universe

Daddy Dragon Guardians Series

Shifters Between Worlds Series

<u>More Shifter Romances</u>

Forever Fated Mates Box Set

Shifter Daddies Box Set

Beverly Hills Dragons Series

Dragons of Sin City Series

Dragons of the Darkblood Secret Society Series

Packs of the Pacific Northwest Series

<u>Early Short Stories</u>

Mated By The Dragon Boss

Claimed By The Werebears of Green Tree

Bearer of Secrets

Rogue Wolf

ABOUT THE AUTHOR

Meg Ripley is an author of steamy shifter romances. A Seattle native, Meg can often be found curled up in a local coffee house with her laptop.

Download Meg's entire *Caught Between Dragons* series when you sign up for her newsletter!

Sign up by visiting www.redlilypublishing.com or Meg's Facebook page: https://www.facebook.com/authormegripley/

www.ingramcontent.com/pod-product-compliance
Lightning Source LLC
Chambersburg PA
CBHW031125130726
47988CB00006B/2233